Books By Janet Lambert
by year of original publication

PENNY PARRISH STORIES
Star Spangled Summer 1941
Dreams of Glory 1942
Glory Be! 1943
Up Goes the Curtain 1946
Practically Perfect 1947
The Reluctant Heart 1950

TIPPY PARRISH STORIES
Miss Tippy 1948
Little Miss Atlas 1949
Miss America 1951
Don't Cry Little Girl 1952
Rainbow After Rain 1953
Welcome Home, Mrs. Jordon 1953
Song in Their Hearts 1956
Here's Marny 1969

JORDON STORIES
Just Jennifer 1945
Friday's Child 1947
Confusion by Cupid 1950
A Dream for Susan 1954
Love Taps Gently 1955
Myself & I 1957
The Stars Hang High 1960
Wedding Bells 1961
A Bright Tomorrow 1965

PARRI MACDONALD STORIES
Introducing Parri 1962
That's My Girl 1964
Stagestruck Parri 1966
My Davy 1968

CANDY KANE STORIES
Candy Kane 1943
Whoa, Matilda 1944
One for the Money 1946

DRIA MEREDITH STORIES
Star Dream 1951
Summer for Seven 1952
High Hurdles 1955

CAMPBELL STORIES
The Precious Days 1957
For Each Other 1959
Forever and Ever 1961
Five's a Crowd 1963
First of All 1966
The Odd Ones 1969

SUGAR BRADLEY STORIES
Sweet as Sugar 1967
Hi, Neighbor 1968

CHRISTIE DRAYTON STORIES
Where the Heart Is 1948
Treasure Trouble 1949

PATTY AND GINGER STORIES
We're Going Steady 1958
Boy Wanted 1959
Spring Fever 1960
Summer Madness 1962
Extra Special 1963
On Her Own 1964

CINDA HOLLISTER STORIES
Cinda 1954
Fly Away Cinda 1956
Big Deal 1958
Triple Trouble 1965
Love to Spare 1967

On Her Own

On Her Own

by Janet Lambert

Image Cascade Publishing
www.ImageCascade.com

MANUFACTURED IN THE UNITED STATES
OF AMERICA

A hardcover edition of this book was originally published by E. P. Dutton & Co. It is here reprinted by arrangement with Mrs. Jeanne Ann Vanderhoef.

First *Image Cascade Publishing* edition published 2003.

Library of Congress Cataloging in Publication Data
Lambert, Janet, 1895–1973.
On her own.

(Juvenile Girls)
Reprint. Originally published: New York: E. P. Dutton, 1964.

ISBN 1-930009-90-9 (Pbk.)

For the twins, Donna and Dale

Dear Readers:

Mother always said she wanted her books to be good enough to be found in someone's attic!

After all of these years, I find her stories—not in attics at all—but prominent in fans' bookcases just as mine are. It is so heart-warming to know that through these republications she will go on telling good stories and being there for her "girls," some of whom find no other place to turn.

With a heart full of love and pride–
Janet Lambert's daughter,
Jeanne Ann Vanderhoef

On Her Own

CHAPTER ONE

"HERE I go to my first day of school," Ginger said, hustling into the kitchen and laying her white purse on the counter. Then she turned in to the small breakfast room where her mother and father sat with the early-morning newspaper and asked, "Do I look neat and dignified enough to pass inspection by the very select private school of Paxton Hill?"

"You look just about perfect to me," her father answered, studying her over the top of his paper.

Stuart Johnston thought no girl in the world could compare with his daughter. Katherine Johnston, who loved her just as much, honestly admitted that Ginger wasn't beautiful by accepted standards. She had soft tan hair that would curl if kept short enough, truly lovely gray eyes surrounded by thick lashes that were too tan to show how long they were, a pert nose sparsely dotted with freckles, and a wide, generous mouth that smiled around an expanse of white teeth an orthodontist had made expensively straight.

Ginger spurned the artificial make-up which most sixteen-year-old girls yearn for or use too lavishly. Her eyelashes were what they were; the sprinkle of freckles was the temporary result of a summer spent outdoors; and except for carefully applied lipstick, her face was the one nature had given her. She was slender, small waisted, and nicely curved, and to her mother she looked exactly like what she was: a happy, well-adjusted high school senior.

"I'm glad you chose the blue-and-white print," Mrs. Johnston said, watching Ginger take a cereal bowl from the cupboard shelf, her round young arms reaching up, her full skirt swaying. Then she sighed, and added, "But I can't help wishing that you were starting off to your own high school back in Cheltham."

"And miss living in this beautiful house and having Daddy become a VIP in business?" Ginger brought her bowl of cornflakes to the table, and as she sat down she teased lightly, "Why, Mrs. Johnston, where's your great sense of adventure? You know perfectly well that we all decided to make this move—one for all and all for one—and I for one am having fun. I'm eager to try a new school."

During the summer the Johnstons had moved from Cheltham, a suburb of Philadelphia, to Vienna, Virginia, just across the Potomac from Washington, D.C. Mr. Johnston had been offered the managership of his firm's big Washington office, and the promotion had seemed too good to refuse. They all had agreed on that. So the dear house that Ginger loved and had grown up in had been sold, and this fine English Tudor dwelling had been bought. It stood handsomely in a woods that was dotted with other equally fine homes, some even larger and more impressive; and while Ginger did her best to show how proud she was of it and of her father's success, she often missed her old and dear friends back home.

Today wouldn't be easy, but neither could it be too bad,

she reflected, spooning sugar on her cereal. It couldn't last over an hour, two at the most, with time only to meet her new classmates and to receive her assignments and the list of books she must buy. Afterward? Well, afterward she would be too busy even to think about whatever the morning had held. This was the day when the whole family of Blakes would be coming for the long Labor Day week end! All of them, including their little dog Heidi; and for three whole days it would be almost as good as living next door to them again.

"Where's Shadow?" she suddenly asked. "I haven't told him today that his best friend is coming," and she jumped up and ran out to the large screened back porch. "Here, Shad. Here, Shadow, boy," she called; and as a brown, shaggy dog rose up out of the bushes and wagged his tail, she said, "Heidi? Where's Heidi? Go find Heidi."

Shadow obliged her by running in circles. He looked under the bushes, barking and wagging his tail, because he remembered the little sausage of a dog that had helped him paw through the trash cans when he knocked them over. Heidi possessed a pedigree, while Shadow had been chosen from the S.P.C.A. Shelter; she was slow-moving and fat, Shadow was bouncy and big-pawed; but they had been pals, and she had followed him about exactly the way Ginger had followed Heidi's owner, Spark Plug. Even after two months in these luxurious surroundings with woods and hidden trash cans, Shadow remembered Heidi. So he barked to call her, then stopped and looked questioningly at Ginger.

"She's coming this afternoon," Ginger said, laughing and holding the screen door open for him. And sitting down to attack her cereal again, she told her parents, "I wish I didn't have to go to that darned old school today. It's such a waste of time. I could meet all the teachers and my classmates on Tuesday when I go on the bus the school sends around. This get-together business sounds awfully silly to me."

"How would you like to drive my Sprite today?" her father asked. "It might give you great distinction to drive up in a foreign car."

"Huh?" Ginger paused with her spoon halfway to her mouth, then grinned. "No, thanks," she said. "I'm not a very confident driver yet—not on these twisting up-and-down roads or on the highways—and I'd feel too little, squashed down between all the big cars. Mom and I've already decided that the station wagon will be safer. But I thank you, anyway."

Mr. Johnston was worried and apprehensive. It had always been so simple when Ginger had started off to her first day of school back in Cheltham, with her best friend Patty Palmer beside her. Sometimes Spark Plug Blake from next door had hooked on, and by the time they reached school, they had collected a whole gang. After eleven years of daily routine, first through the elementary grades and then, later, at the big regional high school, it seemed unfair somehow for Ginger to be so alone. He felt to blame. "I wish your mother could go with you," he said.

"Oh, Daddy, stop being a fuss-budget," Ginger scolded, leaning across the table to him. "I'm not in the first grade, you know, so I don't need to be led in by the hand. And there are only seventeen in the senior class. I'll know them all in two shakes, lots quicker than I did the whole hundred and twenty-five in Cheltham."

Mr. Johnston was a large man with only a tinge of gray in his thick brush of hair, and he looked pleadingly across the table at his wife, who was an older duplicate of Ginger. Something told him they had made a mistake in moving away from Cheltham, and he wanted his wife's reassurance that they hadn't.

"I think Miss Virginia will do very well by herself," Mrs. Johnston told him firmly. "She always has and she always will, so eat your breakfast and hustle off to your office. You have to pay for this expensive school, you know."

Ginger finished a breakfast which didn't want to go down. No matter how much she assured her parents that she looked forward to this day of days, that she was excited and eager to be driving off on her own to a school where she would make new friends, she secretly dreaded it. In the first place, Paxton Hill seemed very far away to a person who had steered a car only to the village and back, and that for only a little over a month. How could she ever, ever get there? And where was she supposed to go when she did?

Paxton Hill was a fairly new school housed in the buildings of an old estate. She had seen it from the outside: a tall brick building painted yellow, and set between two mismatched ones that were half hidden by trees and connected to the main building by walks enclosed in glass. It had looked dull and without charm, especially the registrar's office, where she had spent a painful half-hour presenting her transcript from Cheltham High and answering questions that would determine her suitability to become a Paxton Hill student. But it had a good academic rating and was, heaven knows, expensive.

"Well, here goes," she said, after her father had left and

her watch told her she should be leaving. And she and her mother walked around the house to the white car in the driveway, and she slid under the wheel. The keys were already in the ignition lock, and after she fastened the seat belt, she sat staring at them.

"Are you sure you don't want me to drive you?" her mother asked, suddenly aware of Ginger's grim, determined expression.

"Me? The best driver in the state–and the most cautious?" Ginger turned the key, and shot off unexpectedly with a spurt of gravel. "I'll be home by noon," she called back, all her attention concentrated on making her way down the long curved driveway.

She knew what route she was to follow: past the other houses on the narrow road that dipped and turned like a roller coaster, then right onto Lilac Road and through the village, then right again, then right at the fork of a Y. It seemed to her that she would be making a square and would end up back at home, but for some strange reason she didn't. In a surprisingly short time the semicircular driveway before the main building of Paxton Hill appeared among the trees, and she had to slam on her brake.

"Whoa," she cried, straining against her seat belt and having no time to flip on her direction light before she turned in.

No cars were parked before the school. Where were they? she wondered. Then she saw them through a small grove of trees, in neat rows on a vacant lot. So on she went, direction light blinking properly now, her foot ready to leave the gas pedal as she slid into a wide space between a Porsche and a Cadillac.

Her purse had left the seat when she made her sudden

stop, and bending to retrieve it she found she couldn't. She was still buckled in. "I must be awfully jumpy," she mumbled, releasing herself and carefully removing the car keys. Then she remembered the brake and put that on. The car looked safe. It was much safer than she was, she thought, because it had nothing to do but stand and wait until she came back.

It was pleasant under the trees that were dappled with early September sunshine, but Ginger didn't see any of it. Her feet found a cement walk and trudged dutifully along it while she concentrated on calming the staccato beating of her heart.

A few brick steps took her up to an old-fashioned portico. Beyond it, double doors stood open and she could see into a large square hall that buzzed with activity. First graders, as well as upper classmen, darted about, and Ginger was reminded that this was also an elementary school. A bouncy, pleasant-looking man stood in the center of everything, shaking hands with students, bending over for the small ones and sometimes giving them a pat on the head. He had a narrow black mustache and was almost bald, and he wore a brown sports jacket and gray slacks in an easy, comfortable way. Ginger decided he must belong to the school; one of the teachers, perhaps, since everyone knew him. Then he saw her and came forward.

"Ah, Miss Johnston," he said cordially, holding out his hand. "I'm Dr. Cartwright, the headmaster here. I was sorry to be on leave when you came with your parents for your interview. But come in, come in. You'll find us in quite a hubbub this morning, but we do straighten out, I assure you."

Ginger liked him. He was very different from Mr. Gates,

the principal back at Cheltham High, who seemed quite stern and dignified until you got to know him better. Dr. Cartwright's brown eyes had dancing hazel flecks in them that sparkled like gold and made him look pleasant and warm, as if he would have great understanding of a young person's problems.

"Now let me see," he said, looking about the hall at the different groups of older students who had stopped talking to stare at Ginger. "You're our only new senior, so I must find someone to introduce you about, to instruct you on our way of doing things here. All our teachers have gone to their classrooms, and. . . ." He stopped, thought a moment, and asked, "Have you met your big sister?"

"My—big sister?" Ginger didn't know she had one, so she shook her head. "I haven't heard anything about her," she said.

"Well, mercy on us. There has been a slip-up somewhere, so I'd better pop into the registrar's office and ask about it." He started off, then stopped to explain, "Every student has a big sister or brother—to help them adjust, you know, to advise them and make sure they're happy. The older ones take on the younger, but since you're a senior we had to appoint a girl in your class. Yours was supposed to contact you before now and to be here to meet you, and if you'll excuse me a minute I'll see what the misunderstanding was."

Ginger stood where he left her. The little children had galloped off somewhere, and the older ones, still talking in groups, had stopped looking at her. If there was an extra big sister among them, she didn't come forward. Then, looking along a corridor that extended on from the back of the big hall, she saw a girl detach herself from a flanking escort of three boys and come slowly toward her.

The girl, Ginger thought, having time to watch a reluctant progress, was really something. She had gilt-gold hair that was probably really dark blond or even light brown, and it was upswept in places. One side was strained back to leave an ear looking naked, the other drooped over a cheek, and the whole mess was piled on top of a head that looked too small to hold it. Also, she wore a tight purple skirt, a size too small, and a bright pink blouse with the most plunging neckline Ginger had ever seen off a movie or television screen.

"Hi," she said in a bored voice that was supposed to sound sultry. "I'm Valerie De Camp." And when Ginger answered with unstudied frankness, "I'm Ginger Johnston, and it's nice to meet a classmate," Valerie stopped posing and said, "I was appointed to be your big sister, and I kept meaning to call you up but I forgot to. The summer's so busy, you know."

"Yes, it is." Ginger's six weeks in Laurel Hills had been only intermittently busy: once when her friends from home came for a four-day house party, once when Tim Ford drove down to take her to a dance that turned out badly, and again, just last week end, when Tim and Spark Plug arrived together and spent two days jealously watching each other.

"Umhum. Well, I guess you'd better come with me."

Valerie started off along the corridor, and Ginger fell into step beside her. It was hard to do because Valerie's steps were of necessity mincing, and she was undecided about where she was going first.

"I suppose I ought to introduce you around," she said gloomily, looking at the three boys who still waited for her. "And then I've got to see that you meet the teachers and tell you what stuff you have to buy, and. . . ." She broke off to ask, "You know about the dumb uniforms the school makes us wear, don't you?"

"A little," Ginger answered. "The catalogue said gray pleated skirts, white blouses, and navy-blue blazers with the school monogram on the pocket."

"Yeah." Valerie stopped again to finish the informative part of her duties before they reached the boys, and said, "You can buy the stuff either at Gerber's or at Swanson's. Gerber's is more expensive, but my mother likes it better because she says I don't wear their things out so fast. The little kids, and some of the older ones, too, have to wear the loose pleated skirts because they're fat and bulgy, but any girl with a decent figure can have stitched pleats if she wants them." She studied Ginger as if seeing her for the first time, and said, "You're flat in the stomach so you can have stitched."

"They're the kind I wear most of the time," Ginger agreed. Then, looking at the front and rear bulges of Valerie under the restraining purple, she added, "But it doesn't matter. I can buy one of each."

"You ought to have three. Two jackets, three skirts. And you don't always have to wear a white blouse. You can run in a colored one now and then by pretending your laundry didn't come back, just so they have round collars. Do you remember the name of the stores I told you about?"

"Yes." Ginger didn't need to make a note of them. The

catalogue had already informed her, so she asked, "What else should I know?"

"Search me." Valerie almost looked her seventeen years as she disarranged her too adult coiffure by running a purple-nailed hand across her forehead. "Oh, yes," she said, batting her violet eyes that were richly ringed with mascara. "Minimum make-up after today. That means lipstick and a *little* powder. You really catch it if you overstep. Dig?"

"Sure," Ginger said, wondering why Valerie was in such a strict school.

"Then let's get moving." Valerie minced on again, saying, "We had sixteen seniors until you came along. Eight girls, eight boys. Now you've thrown us. But maybe it's all right because Liza Rysedale never was any good to us and we have to pal around with the juniors anyway. There are twenty-six of them, and we're all so consolidated that I can't see any use being a senior. No special privileges. Just yak, yak, yak, from old Cartwright and Mrs. Pierce, his assistant, about setting a good example. They're nuts. Last year's seniors set us a lousy example."

"How many are there in the whole school?" Ginger asked for something to say.

"Oh, around four hundred, I guess." Valerie looked at the waiting boys, and grinned, either at them or pleased with her next remark, as she said, "Not being a cop, I never bothered to stand outside and count them." Then, having reached the boys, she chose the shortest, tubbiest one to introduce, and said airily, "This is Hal Friedendorfer. He's a whizz at math, and not above helping a pal who needs it." And of a tall, thin boy who had grown too fast, she said,

"Constant Larkins. Only, he isn't that—constant, I mean. He's fickle, so you can call him Con. And this. . . ." Ginger noticed that Valerie had saved the best-looking boy for last and that she slurred over her introduction of him. "Burke Mathews," she mumbled. "Come on, let's get the show on the road."

It seemed to Ginger that the farther they went and the more rooms and teachers they visited, the more students they collected. Valerie, though sloppily exotic, was apparently popular. Most of the students had no last names. They were simply, "Hi, Suse," "Hi, Betsy," or "Cecelia," or "Hey there, Georgie boy." And during the first few introductions she added, "This is Ginger. It *is* Ginger, isn't it?"

"Yes," Ginger said for the fifth time.

She saw the dining room. The crowd that was by now accompanying her trooped with her through the glassed-in runway, and one of them—she thought it was the Betsy one—pointed to all the tables set for eight, and volunteered, "The little kids up to the fifth grade are fed first and put out to play, and every morning menus are passed around first thing. You mark whatever you want, and heaven help you if you change your mind."

"Why?" Ginger asked, accustomed to a cafeteria where students selected their meals before a long steam counter.

"Because old Sully—Miss Sullivan to her face—is the dietitian, and she says she can cook just what we need and save money this way. Boy, does she save it!"

The tour suddenly ended. Ginger had met a few of her teachers and the administrative staff and had the list of the books she would require. Through the dining-room windows she had seen an athletic field with a row of wooden bleachers behind it, and in the far distance a long row of stables and an enclosed riding ring. Nobody had suggested walking out there, but she didn't mind. She hadn't planned to ride. She did wonder where the auditorium and the gymnasium were, however, but hesitated to ask because she had asked so many questions already. They could be in the building they hadn't visited, where someone had said the chemistry lab was. And anyway, she thought with a sigh, she would have nine whole months to wander around in this place.

"You've been awfully nice to me," she said, when they were back in the big center hall again. "Thanks, Valerie, for everything. And all the rest of you, too," she added, to the few who were left.

"Sure, glad to do it." Valerie grinned a gamin sort of grin that didn't go with her hair-do. "Just come to me any time, little sister. Sure you know how to find Gerber's?"

"Oh, yes. It's over at Seven Corners, quite close to the dime store," Ginger answered quickly. Then she hesitated. "I have my car here," she finally blurted out. "If any of you would like to ride over with me—to buy your books and things, I mean."

"We all have transportation." Valerie linked her arm through the tall boy's, the one she had called Burke, and said, "We'll see you on Tuesday. Be good."

"I'll try to. And thanks again. Thanks, all of you," Ginger said, smiling impartially at the group. "I think I'm going to like it here."

She had crossed the narrow porch and gone down the steps when Burke Mathews caught up with her. "You don't have to be in such a hurry," he said, taking her by the arm, exactly as Valerie had taken him. "Where do you think you're going in such a rush?"

"Home," she answered.

"Where's that?"

"Over near Vienna, in Laurel Hills."

"Got a telephone?"

"We had when I left."

Ginger was accustomed to boys, and felt as free and friendly with them as she did with girls, but she didn't like being hooked so tightly to one. Spark Plug might grab her arm, but he usually grabbed both of them to shake her; Tim or Steve might do it to keep her from tripping over something. This business of walking along rubbing shoulders embarrassed her, especially since she had just met this boy. "I've got to hurry," she said inadequately, pulling away and pretending to look at her watch. "Oh, golly, I'm late."

She wanted to skim through the little grove, but Burke kept beside her. "Which is your car?" he asked, as if unaware of the quick way she had detached herself.

"That one."

She pointed to the white station wagon that looked awfully solid and suburban sitting among the foreign cars and convertibles, and felt ashamed of herself for wishing it were her father's Sprite. "Thanks, Burke," she said, taking her keys from her purse. "I'll be looking forward to next week."

"How about that telephone number?" he persisted, opening the car door for her then blocking its closing after she was seated.

"Oh, yes. It's Westmore 8-2669."

"I might give you a ring sometime. Okay with you?"

"Why, yes, I guess so," she answered, wishing he would move his face back.

It was so close to her that she couldn't lean forward to fit her key in the lock, so she kicked off the brake in a businesslike way and turned to lay her purse on the seat. Then, reaching out to start the motor, she made a sweeping motion and her arm flew up and banged him on the chin. "Oh, gosh, I'm sorry," she cried, watching his head jerk up. And while he was backing away she closed the door. "I get sort of nervous when I'm about to drive, you know," she explained. "But once I'm started I'm all right. 'By, and thanks."

She knew he was watching her as she backed out of the parking lot, and she was sure that Valerie stood on the school steps as she passed. No one could miss that purple skirt, not even with eyes focused ahead.

"Whew," she said, glad to be homeward bound, but wishing she had a magic carpet that could waft her in to her own driveway. "That boy's a fast worker."

She poked along for a few minutes, thinking about her morning. To have a big sister seemed so silly. She didn't need one, and was quite capable of adjusting to her teachers and her classmates by herself. The catalogue would tell her the school's rules, and she would obey them. And she didn't need to be led from one classroom to another like a public charge. She could walk with whoever happened to be going her way. A big sister? *Valerie De Camp* a big sister?

The whole idea struck her as childish and amusing, and she began to laugh. "Wait till I tell Spark Plug," she said aloud, and drove faster.

CHAPTER TWO

GINGER shifted to low gear before she started up her driveway. The grade wasn't steep but it had a curve in it, and Shadow was bounding across the lawn to meet her. "Go away," she ordered, stopping the car. "Shoo!" But he only stood looking up at her, his tongue hanging out in a grin.

The house was beautiful, she thought, sitting a moment to appreciate the first view of it that the Blakes would have when they arrived later in the day. It looked enormous, but it wasn't really. A wing, with the double garage built under the big room Spark Plug's sisters would have, was set back a little and went shooting off toward the woods at an angle. This addition made space for a hall to run the width of the house with doors opening into the garage, the library, and the kitchen. A steep back stairway led upstairs from the hall, and tucked in at the end was the small breakfast room.

The house was interesting because it wasn't built in one long, straight line. The living room with its mullioned bay window jutted out beyond the front door that opened into a flagstoned foyer, and in the back, behind the dining room and kitchen, the projecting wall of the long living room on one end and the breakfast room on the other, bricked in the two ends of the screened back porch that had been the Johnstons' delight. Ginger was proud of each square foot of it.

Shadow, tired of waiting unnoticed while she admired her house, trotted off into the cool garage, so she followed along and pulled into her allotted side. Then she hopped out of the car and ran up the few steps to the hallway, opened the kitchen door, and called, "Yoo-hoo. I'm home."

"I'm on the porch, honey," her mother answered. "I heard you drive in, so I brought our lunch out here. Come tell me what happened."

"Okay." Ginger stumbled over Shadow, who had no gentlemanly instincts and was pushing in ahead of her in a great hurry to reach his water bowl, and went out to the porch.

"I don't know what to tell you," she said, flopping onto a redwood chaise longue with green cushions and resting her head against its back. "It was kind of a queer morning."

"In what way?" Her mother took one of the trays from the big round table and set it on a small table beside Ginger. "Didn't you meet other students?" she asked.

"Oh, sure. The place was a madhouse: little kids running around, everybody telling about what a wonderful summer they'd had. I kind of liked the headmaster," she said, picking up a deviled egg and looking thoughtfully at it. "Three or four of the teachers seemed swell, but I didn't get a chance to talk with them." She put the egg up to her mouth, then held it there as she asked, "Did you ever hear of a school assigning big sisters and big brothers to its pupils?"

"No, I can't say I ever did," her mother answered, shaking her head.

"Well, I've got one. Her name's Valerie De Camp."

"What is she supposed to do for you?" Mrs. Johnston asked, ignoring her own lunch.

"Darned if I know." Ginger was absorbed in thought as she ate her egg, but finally she said, "She took me around to the different classrooms, most of them not mine, and introduced me to a lot of kids, only seven of them seniors, and she told me that if ever I get into any trouble I'm to come to her. She'd be a hot one to go to if you got into trouble," Ginger said, remembering Valerie's purple skirt and plunging neckline, her fantastic hair and thick mascara. "But I did gather that she's the leader of Paxton Hill's social set. Boys simply flocked around her."

"Did you like her?" Mrs. Johnston prompted. "That's important. Did you like her?"

"Well—yes, I did," Ginger answered, picking up a cream-cheese sandwich and taking a bite. "That was the funny part of it. She isn't like any girl I've ever known or would choose to know, and she'd make the pseudo-sophisticated Patty Palmer look like a kid in kindergarten, but I'll bet—if you'd wash off the make-up—you'd find an insecure, mixed-up girl underneath." Ginger laughed, and reached for her iced tea before she added, "I'm sure I baffle you, but Valerie baffled me. And then there was a boy," she said. "He was—fresh."

"With Valerie?"

"No, with me." Ginger grinned, then sobered to say, "He latched on to me when I walked out to my car—and I do mean latched—with his arm stuck through mine as if we were pasted together. Burke Mathews was his name, and he said he might call me up sometime. Get that? He *might* call me. He's good-looking in a blond smirky way, but he's not as good-looking as he thinks he is."

"Weren't there any classmates you could really enjoy?" her mother asked, pulling her own tray closer and beginning to eat.

"Well, there was a girl named Cecelia and one named Betsy who were more my type. I don't know their last names, and every time I started to ask them Valerie would begin yakking again and they'd hang on her words as if her silly remarks were absolutely profound. So did everyone else, even that dumb Burke character."

Ginger sighed and stopped making a pretense of eating, as she said, "I wonder what became of that cute girl I met the day we went for my interview. She lived in Falls Church and was named Pamela something but I didn't see her around. She used to go to Friends', in Washington, so I suppose she decided to stay there. Oh, well."

Mrs. Johnston had hoped to see Ginger come in glowing and filled with enthusiasm for the new school. Ginger could be enthusiastic about almost anything, and it hurt her mother to watch her try to hide her disappointment. "Honey," she suggested, "would you like to drive home with the Blakes and have a few days with Patty?"

"Mercy on us, no!" Ginger sat up straight on the chaise longue and said, "You seem to forget that school starts Tuesday. I've got a lot to buy before then, and going in a week late would ruin me. I'm not *that* good a student."

She took up her sandwich again and began nibbling at it, then looked up and smiled her special, eager smile. "Let's concentrate on our three joyous days with the Blake family," she said. "I'll tell all my troubles to old Spark—

he had to start in a big university where he didn't know anybody—and then I'll call up Valerie and ask her to bring some of the gang over tomorrow night. Elston Howard Blake, as a sophomore in college, ought to make impressive bait and establish me as a worldly girl with good contacts. Not that I'm worldly or even semisophisticated," she explained, "but I've had lots of experience at being a hostess."

"Ever since you were nine and uninvited guests ate up every cake I baked," her mother put in, glad to see Ginger's spirits rising enough to plan a strategic campaign.

"Then let's make ready for the Blakes' arrival. What's left for me to do?"

"Everything's done, and you know it," Katherine Johnston said, getting up to take the two small trays. "I'll pop the plates in the dishwasher and you can check the house again if you like. But don't try to squeeze in another vase of flowers," she warned. "We've picked everything that's pickable and I've run out of vases."

"I'm rising to the call of duty." Ginger tossed the rest of her sandwich to Shadow, who had a hollow pit for a stomach, and scattered pieces of ice from her tea that she hoped would keep him busy for several minutes, then gave her mother a hug.

"Everything's dandy," she said, "so stop worrying. I'll get to know these kids in two shakes. Spark Plug will do his best to help me." She paused to look out at the beautiful green lawn with its backdrop of trees before she said, "If we only had Tim here to charm Valerie out of her senses, I know I'd be a true social success." Then she dashed inside to inspect a house that she knew was perfection.

The dining room, inside the French doors, was lovely, with a bouquet of tall gladioli on the sideboard, a bowl of shortened ones on the table. The long living room was so neat that not even one of Shadow's hairs disgraced the large Oriental rug in the center or the two smaller ones at each end. The dark green walls made a beautiful background for the few good paintings her mother had inherited; the grand piano beside the bay window had a bowl of roses on its closed top; every table held some arrangement of flowers, and every chair had its down cushions plumped up and ready to receive an appreciative guest.

"Okay in here," she called, moving up two steps and across the foyer to the paneled library that was equally neat and flowery.

Further inspection took her up the wide center stairway where she was careful not to smudge the banister or the oak-paneled walls, and into her parents' bedroom. Only a small vase of flowers in here, but neat. Next came her own suite that had been originally designed for a family with a child and a nurse, but had now been converted into a sitting room, bedroom, and bath for her. She loved it. The bedroom furniture had been painted white by her father; the sofa and chairs in the sitting room had been the gift of her aunt, the pink chaise longue inherited from her mother and father, who had splurged to buy themselves a new one. More flowers, both in here and in the guest room across the hall where Mr. and Mrs. Blake would sleep.

"Okay," she called down, going into the narrow side hall and opening the door to the room over the garage that Spark Plug had twice occupied, once with Tim Ford and Steve Anderson during the house party, and once last week with Tim. It had held Grandmother Galey's big double bed and a cot then; now it had twin beds bought in an outlet store, and she came back to lean over the stairway railing and ask, "How come everything in here looks so austere and unloved?"

"Little girls don't want to bother with flowers," her mother answered, coming out in the hall and looking up. "And Spark Plug will be bedded down in the basement playroom. You know that."

"Sure. I helped fix it." Ginger ran lightly down the steep steps, saying, "Poor Spark Plug. He'll have a folding cot for a bed, unfinished shelves for his clothes, and Daddy's carpenter bench with a cracked mirror on it for a dressing table. Oh, well, he won't care or even notice." And she ended her tour by saying, "I think the whole place looks lovely. We've cleaned and cooked ourselves to death, so what do we do now?"

"Wait," her mother answered, smiling. "Five o'clock, which is when they said they'd pull in, isn't so far away. Daddy will be home early, and I for one am not against a lazy bath and a nap."

"I am. I'm impatient."

Ginger wished she had something to do, or could telephone someone. Time passed quickly when you were on the telephone, she thought, with your feet propped up on the desk in the library and leaning back in the tall leather desk chair. But who in this lonely place would want to hear her gay lilting voice? Anne Lockwood had gone back to college early, and the ones who were her age, if only she could meet them, hadn't come home from summer jobs or vacations at the shore. The fine community of Laurel Hills, at the moment, was inhabited only by married people with small children. And very few of those.

"Heck," she said to Shadow, who was doing his best to

keep her company, "I might as well be sitting in the middle of a forest."

And then, in her loneliness, she thought of calling Valerie and asking her to round up some friends and bring them over to meet Elston Blake. Elston sounded older and more attractive than Spark Plug. "Valerie's my big sister, isn't she?" she asked Shadow, who was becoming panting-hot by now and wanted to go outdoors. "She was told to rally round and help one Ginger Johnston when she was in dire straits—and this one is dire. How can Spark Plug possibly advise me if he doesn't meet some of my classmates?" Shadow agreed by wagging his tail, so she gave him his freedom.

But Valerie, after Ginger had spent ten minutes looking up all the De Camps in the telephone directory and had received two wrong numbers, wasn't at home. "I'll have her call you back," her mother promised. "What did you say your name is?" And Ginger told her again, and gave her telephone number.

So much for that. There was nothing now to do but find Shadow again and take him for a walk.

Shadow was delighted. They inspected the bloomless flower beds together, looked at the vegetable garden where only tomatoes and a few ears of late corn remained. They wandered over to the brick barbecue where a charcoal fire was laid ready, and stopped briefly before a grouping of iron lawn furniture painted white and topped by a gay red umbrella. Even the woods behind it looked neat because rented goats had eaten off the outer fringe of plaguing honeysuckle. The sloping front lawn was mowed to velvet smoothness and looked too plushy to trample on, so with nothing left to see they wandered back to the porch where Ginger leafed through an old copy of *Life* and Shadow flopped down on the cool flagstoned floor.

Eventually it was four o'clock, and Mrs. Johnston appeared in the dining-room doorway. "Why, honey, you aren't dressed," she said, looking at Ginger's wilted condition. "You know Spark Plug will get here early if he possibly can."

"I hadn't thought of that." Ginger jumped up and tossed the magazine on a table where publications had been neatly stacked. Of course, it landed crooked and open, and she watched her mother close it and lay it on top of the pile. "If Spark Plug's driving," she said, "and he probably is, he won't stop for anything—not even for Dodie, who gets carsick. I'd better hustle." And in the doorway, she asked, "What do you think I ought to put on?"

"Your pink blouse and pink shorts, I'd say," her mother answered. "We're cooking out, and our guests will be so hot from their drive that they'll want to get into something comfortable."

"Umhum." Ginger looked at her mother's crisp blue dress and thought how uncomfortable it must be to grow older and have to look dignified. Then she realized that her mother wore a three-piece playsuit and was ready to slip off the skirt should her guests have brought shorts, and she laughed. "I suppose Daddy will still be dressed like the big executive and it's important for you to match him—for a few minutes at least. Well, I can take a quick shower and change. Spark Plug is sure to look like the dickens."

Suddenly, she was in a great hurry. Her hair, after steaming under a cap in the shower, curled up and stuck out like a little girl's; her white loafers needed cleaning; she couldn't find her pink belt, and had to go down to the laundry room in the basement for it. And it had to be ironed. Lipstick smeared, a nail caught in her zipper and broke, so that when she heard a car in the driveway and went plummeting down the stairs and out the front door she was hotter than she had been all day.

"It's only Daddy," she said, seeking the cool of the porch again. "He looks cooked. I'm going out on the front steps to wait for the Blakes."

"We're all hot," her mother answered, checking her chilled salad in the refrigerator to make sure it had jelled. "Shall we take out some of the canvas chairs and sit under a tree?"

"And look *awful?*"

Ginger shuddered, but seeing her mother's excited face she realized that the Blakes' coming was even more important to her parents than it was to her. "Why, it's your first house party!" she cried, sorry to have been so slow to realize it. "I've had my gang here, but this is the first time you've had a chance to show our terrific house to anybody from home. It's an important event." And she ran down to the garage to take a large bag of ice cubes from her father.

The bag dripped on her when she stuffed it into the basement freezer, but she didn't mind. The wet spots would dry, and should the Blakes arrive before they did, so what? No one would notice. Certainly not Mr. and Mrs. Blake, who would be busy talking, or Dodie and Debbie, who would be glad to be out of the car—or even Spark Plug. It would all be confusion, with her own parents in the center of things.

They sat on the steps. The western sun sank conveniently

behind a stalwart oak tree, and Shadow stretched out in the shade. Stuart Johnston sat rolling up his white shirt sleeves, and there was no sound but the chirping of birds and the hum of late summer insects. Ginger thought they looked like statues in a family group, so she said, "Spark Plug and I sat here and watched for my gang to come. They were late."

"The Blakes won't be," her father answered, getting up and squinting at a green car that took the rolling road as if it knew where it was going. "Here they come."

Dignity was forgotten. Johnstons spilled across the lawn; and when Spark Plug stopped the car before the garage, Shadow was barking in the lead.

People came tumbling out of the car. There was a great deal of hugging and handshaking; and under cover of his mother's soft exclamations about the beauty of the house and his father's booming praise, Spark Plug was able to say to Ginger, "You may think we've come to stay a month from all the stuff Mom insisted on bringing." And then he yelled, "For gosh' sakes, Debbie, don't drag out Heidi's water pan! *Look out!* You're throwing water on everyone. Now you've splashed Ginger!"

"No, she didn't," Ginger said, laughing. "I did it myself before you came. But, honey," she said, pulling Debbie away from the car, "you'd better let Heidi out before Shadow knocks you down."

Heidi was peering uncertainly through the open door and giving sharp, excited barks. She remembered Shadow, but Spark Plug had to tug on her collar to haul her out. Then she and Shadow went tearing around the lawn in the pattern of circles they always made, with Heidi sometimes cutting across to catch up and everyone watching them.

"Here's the cooler with the cake and ham and stuff in it," Spark Plug said, opening the trunk of the car, "and more rose bushes from your old yard that Mrs. Knudson dug up and made us bring. And here's a typewriter that Mom insisted you could use, and a box of old clothes your mother wanted for a rummage sale; and I don't know what this carton is. I'll get to the luggage in a minute."

He looked so hot from having piloted his family such a long distance that Ginger leaned closer to suggest, "Why don't we unpack the rest of the car later? We can either go to the Laurel Hills pool to swim or you can take a quick shower and put on shorts."

"I'll settle for the shower," he said, coming up with a paper bag that held Heidi's cans of special rations. "The kids would yell to go along with us if we went to the pool. I haven't seen you for a week."

"Five days," Ginger corrected.

"Well, I had Tim around all that week end, so it wasn't too good. By the way, he sent you his best," Spark Plug reported honorably. "He'd have detoured down here on his way to Penn State at the first kind word from me."

"I know. He suggested it to me, too." Ginger couldn't resist a little teasing, so she said, "He called up and asked me to come to Penn State to a dance next month."

"Are you going?"

"Now, how could I?" Ginger frowned into his anxious stare. "It's too expensive to fly and it would be an all-day drive—if I were a good driver, which I'm not—so Tim said. . . ." She broke off because there was no sense in telling Spark Plug that Tim planned to come back in

October, when Penn State played Virginia Military Institute, and would take her down to the game. But Spark Plug wasn't satisfied.

"What did he say?" he demanded.

"He said he was sorry, what else? So stop being dopey and worrying about the future."

She slipped her arm through his to pull him away from the car and didn't feel at all as if they were pasted together. His shoulder was several inches above hers, and as they walked along she let her hand slide down his arm. It was a hard, muscular arm, and when her fingers reached his they nestled in a big, capable hand.

She could hear voices inside the house, and although she had planned to take the tour with the Blakes, listening to their pleasure in everything, she now decided against it. "I'll sit out here and wait for you," she said, when they had walked around the end of the garage and reached the isolated lawn furniture. "You're quartered in the basement."

But Spark Plug sat down beside her. "There's no hurry," he said. "I've cooled off now."

"Shall I bring out the pitcher of lemonade?"

"No, thanks." He leaned back and looked at her.

His fine gray eyes, which were his best feature, regarded her soberly. Spark Plug wasn't handsome as Tim was, Tim of the fudge-brown hair and brown eyes. His face was too square, his dark eyebrows too heavy, his black hair too unruly. But he was big and dependable. He had earned his nickname by restoring and selling an old 1914 car he had inherited, and was using the money to pay part of his way through college. Ginger had been his grease monkey all during the years when he was working on the car, sometimes helping but usually devotedly hindering, and he had only recently begun to think of her as a girl. The open devotion to her of Mark Timberlake Ford, III, had never bothered him until this summer. Now it did. It worried him more than he would admit, even to himself.

Tim had always called her "Ginger-cookie" in a light teasing way, so Spark Plug had clumsily set about finding a pet name for her that he could say without feeling foolish. He had tried "old buddy," but lately she had bristled every time he said it. She was tired of being a buddy, it seemed, young or old, so he had unwillingly dropped it and hunted for a new term of endearment.

"Tell me what you've been doing, honey child," he said. And he added before she could speak, "Since Mom talked to you last night, I mean."

"I went to school today," Ginger replied, secretly so pleased and proud of him for wrenching out the new name that she almost reached for his hand again. And she told him everything about her morning, from her big-sister Valerie to the very fresh boy who had escorted her out to her car. "I wish you could meet some of them and give me your opinion," she said when she finished. "I never went to a school like his. We had over a hundred seniors back in Cheltham. We all came from different elementary schools but we didn't have to be introduced around."

Spark Plug was watching a fivesome toiling up the driveway. Four of them were girls from ten to twelve years old, and the fifth was a little fellow who tagged along at the end. "Who are they?" he asked.

"Oh, Mom saw Mrs. Lattimore in the supermarket

yesterday and told her about Dodie and Debbie coming to visit, so I suppose her kids and the Yardleys have come to see them." Ginger half rose, then dropped back again, realizing that the straggling band was headed for the front door and her mother could do the presentation honors. "They have on bathing suits," she said, "so I guess Dodie and Debbie will beat us to the pool. We probably won't see your sisters much before they leave. I wish this dumb place grew some friends my age."

"Okay, go on and describe this Valerie De Camp and Burke whatever-his-name is. I'd like to meet 'em."

"I'd like to have you."

Ginger respected Spark Plug's judgment, so she said with a sigh, "I did call her up to ask her to bring some of her friends over tomorrow night, but she wasn't home. Her mother said she'd have her call me back."

"Okay."

Spark Plug was happy to be alone with Ginger, but he knew she depended on him to meet her classmates and pass on them. She always had. It went all the way back to the third grade when Ginger had given a poor child her roller skates and one of her best dresses, and had been snubbed by the ungrateful recipient from then on. And there were the misfits she was always dragging home with her because she felt sorry for them and was sure she could rehabilitate them by showing them a pleasant home life. Spark Plug had been the one to rescue her from her own bountiful hospitality and send them packing. "Do you expect Valerie to call you back?" he asked, knowing girls better than Ginger thought he did.

"Well, why shouldn't she?" Ginger asked, surprised.

"She's my big sister, isn't she? Why, I might be in terrible trouble for all she knows."

"And if she doesn't, what do you plan to do?"

"I don't know. Skip it, I guess." Spark Plug was as direct in his methods as a surgeon, always cutting straight to the heart of a trouble, no matter how much a person bled in the process, so she said uncomfortably, "I don't want to seem—pushy."

"You wouldn't. If I were new in a town and met some Joe, I wouldn't hesitate to call him up and ask him to mess around with me."

"Is that what you did in college?" Ginger asked sweetly. "Is that the way you met Mayo Thatcher?"

"Now, cut that out." Spark Plug hated to dwell on the time last spring when he had felt so romantic about Mayo that she had believed they had an understanding and so had made a summer trip to his home town. Ginger had helped him show Miss Thatcher that he was nothing more than a friend, and he still felt embarrassed about it. The Mayo Thatcher phase had died off in a few weeks, but Tim's devotion to Ginger had been going on for three years.

"Listen," he said, having observed that she always looked meek when he spoke with authority, "I'm not going to fight with you. I've only got until Monday, and I'm not going to waste my time fighting."

"Yes, sir." Ginger's teasing vanished and she grinned. "Come on, you big lug," she said. "I don't want to fight, either, so let's go in and call my big sister again." And she pulled him to his feet.

CHAPTER THREE

VALERIE still hadn't come home. She didn't call back, not during dinner or while Ginger and Spark Plug were at a drive-in movie. It was at nine o'clock the next morning, when the Blakes and Johnstons were finishing an informal breakfast on the porch, that the telephone rang.

"Hello," Ginger answered the ring, not expecting it to be Valerie and surprised that it was.

"My mother said you expected me to call you," Valerie said in a voice that sounded like an early snowfall. "You aren't in trouble already, are you?"

"Oh, mercy, no." Ginger gave a little laugh to make things seem friendlier. "I have a house guest, Elston Blake, who's a sophomore at Purdue University—out in Indiana, you know—and since I'm so new here and don't know anybody, I was wondering if you could bring some of the Paxton Hill crowd over tonight. Elston," she explained, "will be here until Monday, so either tonight or tomorrow would be all right."

"I'm all dated up," Valerie returned flatly, without tacking on so much as "I'm sorry." "I have a gang coming here tonight and Burke and I are going on an all-day picnic. Tomorrow's filled up, too."

"Oh." Ginger was the one to say she was sorry. She felt foolish standing there with the telephone in her hand, especially as Spark Plug had come into the library and was looking quizzically at her.

"I'll see you at school Tuesday," Valerie said coolly. "If there's anything else you want—advice about school, I mean—give me another call. Is there?"

"No, thanks."

Ginger was so embarrassed that she wanted to run as far as she could, all the way to Cheltham if need be, but she replaced the receiver and said, as best she could manage, "I never should have called her. I know that now."

"But you didn't five minutes ago," Spark Plug reminded. "You thought she was pretty far out but you liked her. Why couldn't she round up her friends and come over?"

"She's having a party of her own," Ginger answered miserably, "at her house."

"And she didn't ask us to come and join on? My gosh," Spark Plug said disgustedly, "you weren't crying to crash in, you have a date of your own. Any girl I know would have said, 'Come over and join us, if you've got your own date.' "

"I guess Valerie wouldn't." Something troubled Ginger, far back in her mind, but she couldn't quite place what it was, so she said, "Valerie wasted a lot of time on me yesterday and didn't seem to mind. She was really friendly." And then a faint trickle of light filtered through and burst like a thousand-watt bulb. "I'll bet it was Burke!" she cried. "Valerie thinks I'm a snatcher. I'm not, and I never have been," she protested. "I couldn't help it because Burke walked out to the car with me. I didn't want him, and if Valerie thinks. . . ."

"Stop babbling." Spark Plug cut her off, even though he knew she was right. "And stop jumping to conclusions. Why would you want Burke, if he's the make-out type you say he is?"

"I don't. I just told you. But perhaps Valerie thinks I do."

"Well, the others won't. All the other kids you met will have sense enough to see that you couldn't help yourself."

"I hope so."

Ginger walked slowly past him out of the library. She felt humiliated and ashamed. Not about Burke, because, as she had told her mother and Spark Plug, she couldn't avoid the unfortunate episode with him, but because she had given Valerie the opportunity to embarrass her. "What shall I say to them on Tuesday?" she asked, backing against the newel post and looking up at Spark Plug miserably.

"Nothing. Just skip it and be friendly with everybody," he advised. "You're always friendly, so just put a little extra effort into it. With everyone," he repeated, "especially the girls."

"Umhum, I'll try."

She turned to watch the rest of the Blake family coming down the stairway. They were off for a day of Washington sight-seeing, and Debbie and Dodie were chattering excitedly. She wanted to be as enthusiastic as they were, but no words would come out past the lump in her throat, so she simply said, "Have fun," and bolted for the back porch.

She supposed they left. Voices in the hall ceased, and

eventually Shadow came trotting around the end of the garage, followed by a disconsolate Heidi. She could hear Spark Plug talking with her father in the garage, her mother putting dishes in the dishwasher. All the sounds were so clear that she could tell the difference between a cup and a plate being placed. She strained to hear to keep from thinking. "There go the spoons," her mind said. "Now Daddy's pulling a board out from behind the ones he keeps for spares, and Spark Plug's rattling the jar of nails." And all the time while her ears attentively singled out the different sounds, her heart kept telling her, "You've ruined everything. You've made yourself afraid to face your first day of school."

There was nothing she could do about it. She couldn't call Valerie back as she would Patty, and say, "Listen, Valerie, please don't think I was trying to crowd in. I wasn't. It's just that I wanted Spark Plug to meet some of the kids I'll be going to school with, that's all. He's been my friend ever since we were little, and he's such a swell guy. And as for that business with Burke. . . ." No, she couldn't. There was nothing she could say that would influence Valerie. It would all have to wait until Tuesday when she could try to make some sort of reasonable explanation. Tuesday seemed a long way off, blocked by the Saturday, Sunday, and Monday that she had so looked forward to.

She might as well join the others, she decided. Sitting here on the porch, moping and being scared, didn't help. Neither did blaming herself. It was better to forget it and enjoy the week end.

Her mother was turning on the dishwasher when she

went through the kitchen, and she looked around to ask, "Is Spark Plug going to take you to buy your uniforms or do you want me to go?"

"He said he would."

"Then get a check from Daddy and fill it in for whatever you need."

"Thanks, Mom."

Ginger went across the hall and down the steps to the garage. Spark Plug had selected some screws from the jar and was laying them on the fender of the Sprite; her father was holding up the board that would eventually become a shelf for cans of paint and small garden tools, and she said, timidly for her, "I do hate to interrupt your work but I'll have to have one of the cars to go buy my things for school."

"Be right with you." Spark Plug actually looked as if he were glad to give up work he enjoyed doing, and he swept the screws into the palm of his hand. "I might buy a couple of iron braces while I'm out," he said to Mr. Johnston, in defense of his hurried departure. "They'll be quicker to put up than the wooden ones we were going to make."

"They would, at that." Mr. Johnston felt in the pocket of his carpenter's apron for the check he had made out earlier, and complained ruefully as he handed it to Ginger, "I thought this was too good to be true. I get myself a fine carpenter and then lose him to a pretty girl."

"I'll stay if you want me to, sir," Spark Plug told him quickly; but he only grinned and winked.

"Take the Sprite," Mr. Johnston said. "I'll need its half of the garage to saw in. Go on. Scoot. Maybe I'll just rest myself on the porch until you come back."

Ginger knew he wouldn't, but she didn't tell Spark Plug. She simply got in the low bucket seat of the little car, pulled in her full pink skirt so she could close the door, and watched Spark Plug slide into the driver's seat.

"Know where we're going?" he asked, after he had backed the Sprite out of the garage and turned around in a very small space.

"Of course. To Gerber's. It's over in a big shopping center and I can even direct you. You turn left instead of going through Vienna."

"Yes, madam." Spark Plug gave her one of his nice smiles and said gently, "You'd better put that check in your purse. It's made out to cash and isn't filled in, you know."

"I won't lose it. I'd like to tear it up, though." Ginger looked down at the check she was hiding in a special little zippered pocket in her white leather bag, and said, "I'd like to tear it into a thousand pieces and never show up at the darned old school."

"Not come Tuesday, you wouldn't," he answered, as the Sprite took rolls and dips in a bouncy way. "You're no coward, and don't let anybody say you are."

"*I* say it. I'm scared green. I'm even afraid I'll meet some of my classmates in that store."

"Valerie, in particular?"

"No, not Valerie, or even Burke Mathews, because they've gone on a picnic. But I'm sure I was well hashed over last night, and if I see a single senior I'm going to take off at a run."

"With me around?" Spark Plug reached out and patted her knee. "We'll look at ladies' ready-to-wear," he said, trying to tease her into smiling, "and pretend we're buying your trousseau."

But when they reached the large department store that was spread out, all on one floor, he tried to back out. They had passed a display of costume jewelry, a cosmetic counter with every conceivable aid to feminine beauty, a lingerie department that embarrassed him by its open display of what his mother always laughingly referred to as "unmentionables." And when they arrived at last in a cul-de-sac that dealt in the dull uniforms of different schools, and found it empty, he watched Ginger walk purposefully up to a counter, and suggested hopefully, "I might as well go back to that hardware store we passed. You'll be trying on stuff for at least an hour, won't you?"

"I don't have to try anything on," she returned, heartened by the privacy of the place. "I'll simply buy three gray wool skirts, size ten, two cotton ones, and two thirty-two-sized jackets. We can go to the hardware store while they sew the monograms on."

"Okay, if that's the way you want it." Spark Plug leaned against a pillar, protectively acting as a lookout while she gave her order, held a skirt against herself, measured, tried on a jacket, and wrote her check. Then, even while he wondered if he could dodge coming back for the jackets, he took the box Ginger handed him and obediently followed her out.

"Women's stores," he grumbled when they were on the sidewalk again, stopping to hoist the box under his arm as if it were a leather brief case and not a pink-and-white-striped affair with large letters saying GERBER'S, and in finer, flowing print, *The store women love.*

Ginger felt happier—a little, but not much. She had bought the clothes she would wear to her doom on Tuesday; she had run into no one from Paxton Hill; and if she could just send Spark Plug back alone for the jackets. . . . She knew she couldn't. One look at him told her that. He had brought her and had stood patiently by, ready to perform any act she might ask of him. Much like a trained bear in a circus, she thought. And now he was waiting for his reward, which would be the trip to the hardware store. She sighed, but she accepted it, and went with him into his male world of knives, lawn mowers, hammers, and bolts.

Brackets, it seemed, came in all sizes, like skirts. Spark Plug measured, rejected, and finally selected six that looked exactly like any of the others to her. Then he bought a can of white paint and a brush that was made of badger's hair, even though she pointed out that a nylon one was much cheaper. And he happily topped the whole thing off, like adding whipped cream to a chocolate sundae, by buying a box of decals that would colorfully identify whatever jars and boxes her father planned to put on his shelf.

"Gosh, that was fun," he said, when they emerged into the sunlight an hour later, Spark Plug carrying a bulky, plainly wrapped package, Ginger swinging her Gerber's box by its pink string. "I'll put this stuff in the car and meet you at the parking lot."

"Oh, dear!" Ginger was tense again. "What if I go back to the store alone and some of the kids are in there now?" she asked in a quavery voice. "We were early before, but it's almost noon now."

"Okay." He knew when to give in, but he compromised, "I'll stand just inside the door. If you signal for me I'll hustle back to you, but I don't want to plow through that mess of nightgowns and things again if I don't have to."

Ginger looked at him thoughtfully. She stood swinging her box and looking for almost a minute before she said, "I didn't like going to the tailor's with you last year, either, when you had your father's tuxedo cut down to fit you. There wasn't a thing between you and me but a screen, and the tailor kept talking about your waistline and taking in the crouch."

"Crotch," he corrected.

"Well, whatever it was, your mother sent me there to make sure you had the thing altered so you could go to a dance."

"So I could take you, you mean," he growled. "You wanted to go to the darn thing—I didn't."

"Well, anyway, I did what I'd been told to do. I stuck to it until I was sure you'd look like the rest of the boys. And," she retorted hotly, "I was only fifteen. You're darned near twenty and you act like a baby."

"I'm nineteen and three months. And six days," he added honorably, wishing Ginger had normal eyes instead of such big gray ones. They always tore common sense right out of him, as if she were pulling on his heart with a rope. "Okay, you win," he said with a sigh, and he actually took her box back as they walked the length of the store again.

Valerie really was there this time, in person. Not with Burke, but with two other girls, and Spark Plug could understand both her and Ginger's startled surprise. Valerie was supposed to be off on a picnic.

"Oh—hi," Valerie said weakly, while one of the girls added a less-embarrassed, "Hello." The third, unaware that drama was taking place behind her, went on looking at a blouse.

"Hello," Ginger said in return.

She did it in an easy way that made Spark Plug proud of her, but Valerie went on staring at them both as if they were Martians. Her face was unbecomingly flushed and her mouth stayed open.

"This is Elston Blake I told you about last night," Ginger said, breaking the tableau. "Elston, this is Valerie De Camp and Cecelia—I don't think I know your last name, Cecelia."

"It's Carpenter," Cecelia said, making the best of a bad business. "And that's Tina Upton over there, buying out the store." Then she gave a tug at Valerie's rigid arm. "Come on," she said loudly. "You know Mother's parked outside waiting for us. She's in a hurry."

"Oh, sure." Valerie came to with a start. The flush faded from her cheeks and she said, "Besides, I have a date." And she snapped, "Tina, are you coming?"

Tina, one of the seniors at Paxton Hill, hadn't met Ginger, but she had heard all about the episode with Burke and the telephone call, so she dropped the blouse as if it had burst into flames. "Wait for me," she said, hustling after the other two who were already on their way. Then, either as a kindness or from training, she stopped to say, "It's nice to know you, Ginger, and I'll see you at school on Tuesday."

Valerie and Cecelia had merely said good-by and hustled out.

"Well!" Spark Plug stared after the three fleeing girls. A store was much too public a place for a discussion of their behavior, so he simply said in a low tone, "We'll talk when we get outside," and went over to the puzzled saleswoman to ask for Ginger's jackets.

Ginger stood where he left her, numbed and miserable. She knew, just as surely as if a line of pickets had marched by her, that the word had gone about and that she was to be boycotted at school.

"Why?" she asked Spark Plug when they were on the sidewalk again, trudging through the hot sunshine to the Sprite. "Why should the whole school be mad at me?"

"Gosh, I don't know." He carried all the packages now, proudly, as if her two striped boxes were the red, white, and blue flags of the United States, a brave display. "That girl's nuts, honey child," he said, waiting while she slid into her seat, then laying their purchases on the small shelf behind her.

"But she's powerful." Ginger waited until he was beside her to say, "She can ruin me, Spark Plug."

"That dizzy blonde? Don't you believe it." He started the motor, then let it idle while he wondered when he had ever been so mad. He wanted to find Valerie De Camp and punch her right in the middle of her whitewashed nose. But you couldn't paste a girl, reason told him. Girls were fragile creatures who were allowed to be obnoxious because they were girls. Most of them took advantage of their blessed estate, and loved it. But Ginger didn't. Ginger, except for her big eyes that could pulverize a block of cement, was amenable and sweet. She was no politician, he knew that; she wasn't even good at pretense, because she was too honest and had ideals. She was—well, she was Ginger, and he loved her because she was the kind of girl she was.

"Aren't we going?" she asked in a small voice, leaning forward to look at his set face. And she added, "It doesn't do any good to be mad. I'm here, and here I'll have to stay. I made a mistake yesterday, and even though I wouldn't have had it happen for the world, I'll have to prove to Valerie that I'm not a snatcher."

"That's not the whole trouble." Spark Plug shook his head, and said, "Valerie has run this school so long that she thinks she's the queen. That brassy-looking dimwit senses danger to her empire."

"From me?" Ginger let laughter bubble out. It was weak but it was laughter. "I'm no threat to anyone," she said, and meant it. "All I want is to be the seventeenth member of the senior class, sitting nicely at my desk and trying to like the darned old school."

"I'd better call you up Tuesday night and see how you make out."

"Oh, will you?" The car swung out of the parking space and threw her against him, as she asked again, "Oh, Spark Plug, will you really call me all the way from Purdue?"

"You bet I will," he answered. "And if you can't take Paxton Hill, maybe you'd better go up to Patty's and finish your year at Cheltham High."

"I'll take it," she vowed, sitting up straight again. She was grimly determined now, and was saying through clenched teeth, "Nothing or nobody is going to make me quit. I'm going to this dumb school to get an education—and, by golly, I'll get it!"

CHAPTER FOUR

HAVING resolved to let nothing that might happen at Paxton Hill dismay her, the week end became incredibly short. Debbie and Dodie had been taken into a younger Laurel Hills group and were rarely seen, even at mealtime. Once they drove up to the house in a pony cart, and once in a small wagon pulled by two enormous goats that were named Huntley and Brinkley, but off they went again. Mr. and Mrs. Blake were completely happy, whether they went somewhere to lunch or simply stayed home with the Johnstons and played bridge, and Spark Plug was so helpful that Ginger thought he must be taking some kind of pep pills.

The shelf in the garage was finished and painted, and she had been allowed to sit on a stool and transfer decals to all the quart jars and wooden boxes. She tired of it in time, and thought disgustedly, and a little nostalgically, too, that this was much like the days back in Cheltham when Spark Park had grunted to her from beneath his old car. She had handed him wrenches then; now she left her work to give him a hammer, but his general conversation was the same. Whether under a car or topped by a shelf, he still mumbled orders to her through a mouthful of screws. But by Sunday evening his rapport with the shelf and a splendid rack for fishing rods was ended, and he announced that what was left of his visit would belong to her.

"Anything special you'd like to do?" he asked, coming up from his basement bedroom, showered and wearing his best cord suit. "Dinner somewhere by ourselves, maybe, and dancing in some night club?"

Ginger, sitting on the porch in the shorts and shirt she had worn all day, stared up at him in surprise. "Well, goodness," was all she could think of to say.

"I don't mean anything too swank," he hastened to add. "Not a place where the cover charge is twenty-five bucks, but just a nice, medium-priced joint with a youthful atmosphere and a good band."

"I don't know any." Ginger rubbed her hands over her bare knees, and sighed. She would like to go dancing with Spark Plug. He wasn't the world's best dancer, but he had a sweet way of resting his cheek against her hair.

"Tim gave me the name of a place," he said. "It's a favorite college hangout, and he plans to take you there when he comes down but he let me have it first. It's called The Baton, and he gave me directions on how to find it."

"I've heard of it. Melanie Lockwood and the boy she's pinned to go there all the time."

Ginger kept nodding her head up and down while she wished Melanie could be at The Baton to see her walk in, but Spark Plug thought she was deciding whether she would rather go with him or wait for Tim the Explorer to take her. "Well, make up your mind," he said, speaking more gruffly than he meant to. "Do we eat dinner with our folks or do we go off on our own?"

Ginger's big eyes flicked up to his. "Do you want to go?" she asked. "Or are you just feeling sorry for me and trying to be nice?"

"Oh, for gosh' sakes!" Spark Plug scowled then and threw up his hands in a frustrated way that looked, to her, like disgust. "I asked you to go," he said. "Now make up your mind."

Ginger sat for several more moments in silence. Spark Plug had never done anything like this. A crowded hamburger joint after a dance was the best he had ever offered before. Sometimes he had invited her to dinner at his house, but his mother had cooked the dinner and Ginger and the whole family had helped with the dishes. Even the corsages that he had been duty bound to send her when he took her to a dance had been selected and paid for by his parents. To spend fifteen or twenty dollars on her, or maybe even thirty? It didn't make sense.

She looked straight at him as she tried to figure out whether his expensive gesture was being prompted by pity for her or by jealousy of Tim. He looked back, so worried, so waiting, that something inside her melted and spread like a warm coating of molasses over her heart. Dear Spark Plug, she thought. He worked every summer to earn extra money for college. He worked so hard and was so frugal. If he had made up his mind to do this, to take her out in such a grand way, he must want to do it very badly. "I—I. . . ." She swallowed and had to take a deep breath before she could say, "I'd love to go. Really, I would."

"Then hop up and get ready. I'm dressed to the teeth, so do you have anything fancy enough to match me?"

"I have a dreamy white embroidered organdy," she said. "Very full in the skirt, scooped out at the neck, no sleeves, and. . . ."

"I remember it. I like it." He caught her by her elbows as she came past him, and stood holding her and looking down into her glowing face. "This will be a night to remember," he said. "It's the first time I ever really wanted to take a girl out and show her off."

"Well, don't get the habit," Ginger retorted. "It's expensive, and I wouldn't like to think of you showing off other girls. Stick to your fraternity dances." And then she said, "I suppose you know that our parents have stopped playing bridge in the living room and are watching us. You've got an iron grip on my elbows so they probably think we're fighting again."

"Nope, Mom's pleased." He still kept his hold on her arms, but he said, "Just this morning she asked me, 'Elston why can't you be nicer to Ginger? You treat her like a sister.' Now she'll know I don't. I wouldn't stay clamped to a sister."

"Or even to an old buddy?" she asked, teasing.

"Yes, to my buddy, I would. You see," he told her soberly, "even though I've called you honey child this summer, you'll always be my buddy." And to his surprise she stood on tiptoe and kissed him on his cheek.

Her path to the front stairway didn't lead through the living room, but she detoured and stopped beside the bridge table. "Spark Plug is the dearest boy," she told the four who looked up at her. "He's going to take me out on a *very expensive* evening. Isn't it super?"

Mrs. Blake smiled in a pleased, proud way, but Mr. Blake

laid down his cards, sat back in his chair, and said, "You don't mean it!"

"I do." Ginger knew he was only pretending to be overcome by his son's sudden largess, so she leaned across the table, and whispered, "We're going to be all dressed up and blow the works. And we're going to *dance!*" she added dramatically. Then, without waiting to enjoy the reaction her words would surely bring, she skipped out and took the stair steps two at a time.

She and Spark Plug chose to drive the Sprite because a low-slung foreign car seemed better suited to their mood of gay adventure than either a family sedan or a station wagon. It looked so rakish and as if it were accustomed to being parked outside a night club. So Ginger tied her hair down with a scarf, and they headed for the Chain Bridge and a more sophisticated part of Washington than either of them had ever visited.

A liveried doorman was waiting under the marquee of the smartly lighted restaurant, and a parking attendant hovered nearby. Ginger's frothy skirts came out of their compact space unwrinkled, her curls still in place; Spark Plug, with the easy gesture of a magician, caused the car to vanish. The magician might use a wand, but Spark Plug's hand held a dollar bill. It also held one for the doorman, and slipped five more to the maître d'hôtel, who came pleasantly to life and escorted them to a small table that bordered the dance floor.

"Wow," Ginger said, impressed. "Tim must have really coached you."

"Don't you think I know my way around?" Spark Plug glowered at her above a menu so large that she could see only his eyes, and she shook her head.

"*I* don't," she said, "so why would you?" And then she shrugged, and added, "But perhaps you took Mayo Thatcher to Chicago, and learned."

"Ginger!" There was no "buddy" or "honey child" mixed in with that short word. Spark Plug laid the menu down and asked stiffly, "Would you like to dance?"

"N-no." Ginger could only shake her head in a miserable way. She had ruined the evening! Spark Plug never displayed open jealousy of Tim, yet she was always harping on Mayo. "I'm sorry," was all she could say. And she reached across the table to him, one rounded arm on each side of a small, dim lamp. "It's just that I've never seen you like this before, worldly and sure of yourself," she said softly. "You don't act like Spark Plug because you're being so—so *Elstonish.*"

"If you dance with me, I will," he answered, standing up. "I'll be the same old elephant who used to step on your toes."

"Please do." Ginger slipped easily into his arms and felt the familiar pressure of his shoulder against her cheek.

Spark Plug wasn't a smooth, standing-up dancer. Back in Cheltham she had constantly protested, "Stop *leaning* on me." Now she liked it. He still held himself in a golfer's putting stance, but there was no weight behind it now, and his feet didn't so much as bump her white sandals. He was smooth. He really got about, missing other dancers by a fraction of an inch, and he didn't seem to look where he was going, either. He simply moved with a surety that amazed her. That's what college does for you, she thought, wishing she were older and going to one. Then he leaned back and smiled at her. "I'm happy," was all he said.

Ginger wasn't sure what she ate, or if she ate at all.

Spark Plug ordered magnificently: shrimp cocktails, steaks —done medium rare as they both liked them—tossed green salad, and baked Alaska for dessert. She didn't know he had ever heard of baked Alaska—ice cream topped by a frothy meringue and brought in flaming. She knew, because her mother had tried to make one once and her father had had to put out the fire. And between courses they danced. They danced off and on for four short hours. And they talked. They talked about themselves, about Ginger's stuffy school, about Spark Plug's chances of either landing a good job when he graduated or going on to take his master's in engineering. They even talked about Shadow and Heidi, about Tim and Mayo, about the past, the present, the future, and about what fun they were having. And they left in a happy daze of pleasure, assuring each other that such an evening could never be repeated, not if they lived to be ninety.

Spark Plug summoned the Sprite by using the same sure magic that had made it disappear, and suddenly they were homeward bound. His arm couldn't be around her now; his face wasn't smiling at her across a softly shaded lamp. Ginger felt so far from him that she slid down in her seat and rested her cheek against his shoulder for closeness. "Tonight will never come again," she said sadly. "Never, never, never."

"But others will." He reached for her hand, lifted it to the wheel and kept it under his as he said thoughtfully, "One night, no matter how perfect it is, doesn't make our lives, honey child."

"You don't like that name for me much, do you?" she asked, lifting her head.

"Yes, sometimes." He was silent while he drove for several lighted blocks before he went on, "I like it, all right. It suits you, and yet it doesn't—quite. You're lots more than a honey child. You're sweet, just like it implies, and childish, too, sometimes, but you're so *much more.*"

"Like—what 'buddy' means?"

"Yeah. I couldn't ever think of falling in love with a girl who wouldn't be a buddy to me. Maybe you'd call it a friend, a pal, a wife, but whatever it is, it holds something for me. When I marry, no matter how wonderful you—I mean the girl is, she'll have to be my buddy."

"Then let's go back to the old name. I want to be that, too, to my husband. And I want my husband to be that to me. Buddies. Loving, trustful buddies."

She felt his hand squeeze hers and his shoulder move ever so little so she could rest more comfortably against it. The night was lovely, soft and lovely, and she dropped her head down to the place where it fitted so comfortably.

CHAPTER FIVE

IT SEEMED impossible that the week end could be over, that the Johnstons were once again standing with the Blakes in the driveway, saying good-by this time instead of giving a joyous welcome.

"It was perfect," Mrs. Blake said, caught between departure tears and a smiling memory. "Dodie, Debbie, hop in the back seat and take Heidi with you. Don't fill her water pan *now!*" she cried, taking a Thermos from Dodie and setting it on the floor of the car. "And give her more room. We won't be crowded going back without Elston, so move over. Oh, *Heidi!*" she wailed. "Oh, for heaven's sake!"

Heidi, torn between love for her family and another romp with Shadow, had left the car in a scrambling leap and landed on her nose at Spark Plug's feet. He picked her up and hugged her, let her lick his face and yelp with excitement, then handed her back to Debbie and closed the car door.

"Now, don't miss your plane, son," his father said, turning from his last good-byes to give Spark Plug's hand a quick, brief press. "You're all set for money, aren't you?"

"Oh, sure, Dad. I'll be in Lafayette about the time you get home, and I'll call you. Just to make sure that you're as good a holiday driver as I am," he added, thinking that a little levity might lessen the tension of this parting. "Don't let Mom distract you by saying, 'Oh, look at those cows over there' and 'See that pretty farmhouse.' And don't pay any attention to the back-seat quarreling."

"I never do that," his mother protested indignantly, and from the car came shouts of, "We never fight." Then Dodie shrieked, "Debbie, for Pete's sake move *over!* You don't have to sit on *me.*"

"And on this happy family note we now depart," Mr. Blake said, sliding in to his place and watching his wife give more hugs before she scooted around to hers.

Doors slammed, the car moved, and Ginger ran beside it to call, "Don't worry about Spark Plug. I'll take him to his plane. Good-by, and come back soon."

"Well, peace descends," Spark Plug said as they walked around the garage to the back porch, but Ginger knew he didn't mean it.

He was fond of his family in an undemonstrative way that the Blakes took for granted, and he wouldn't see them again until Thanksgiving, if then. From now on, his life would be separate from theirs, as a son's usually is after he leaves home to go to college. He would have a living to make after he graduated, and would have to go wherever his work as an engineer might take him.

"Are you all packed?" she asked, cupping her hand in his as they walked the well-worn path.

"Yep."

"Would you like a sandwich or a glass of milk, or something?"

"After the late lunch we had? No, thanks. My plane takes off at six, and by losing an hour in time difference, we should be in Indianapolis by eight, so we ought to be served dinner. If I don't miss my bus," he said, "I should be back at Purdue by nine, central time. It seems queer, doesn't it?"

"Umhum." Ginger was glad to see her mother and father on the porch. She had one special task she must perform before Spark Plug left, so she said, "I'll be back in a minute," and left him with them while she ran upstairs.

She had something to find and return. She knew exactly where to look, so she lifted a pile of silk scarves from a drawer in her dresser and took out a folded, slightly tear-soiled white handkerchief. Once it had belonged to Spark Plug, but the tearstains on it were hers. Inside, when she laid back the well-creased folds, was his fraternity pin: the one he had tricked her into taking, the one that, carefully hidden, had pricked her cheek when she pressed the handkerchief to it as he drove away, the one that had so infuriated her at his duplicity that she had run after his vanishing car, shouting and stamping her feet. The pin belonged with him, in college. Knowing that, she knew what she was going to do.

"I'd like to keep you," she said, looking down on what Spark Plug had told her was his most treasured possession, "but I can't. You belong on a college campus, not hidden away in a drawer. Perhaps, someday, if Spark Plug goes on feeling about me the way he does now, and if I feel the same way about him, I can wear you—openly and proudly. Until then, good-by."

She sighed, and opened the safety catch on the little pin. She would keep the handkerchief. She had to. It had sopped up so many tears, and would always be ready for the ones to come.

Clutching the pin in her hand, she went to the desk in her sitting room and took out a sheet of paper and an envelope. What to write? *I'm sorry?* That said so little, not anything about the way she truly felt. Something silly, perhaps, like *I'm getting the last laugh?* She wasn't. She wasn't laughing at all, inside. She looked at the pin again, and, hurried because her last hour with Spark Plug was slipping away, she scribbled hastily, *Please understand. This way, the pin and I are both with you.* Then she ran back to her bedroom to find the lace-trimmed handkerchief her aunt had given her for Christmas.

The little pin was concealed in the handkerchief with the note, the envelope sealed, and she went tiptoing down two flights of stairs like a burglar.

Spark Plug's manly leather suitcase lay open on the cot, and she hid the envelope inside one of his clean white shirts. It was the only safe place she could think of, because he might suspect her of trickery and so take a quick look in the pocket where his neckties were.

"I guess we ought to start," she said, coming back to the porch, trying to look innocent and as if she had just left to comb her hair and apply fresh lipstick. "Daddy, if Spark Plug brings out the wagon will you go down and carry up his luggage?"

"I'll get it." Spark Plug had the look of a doubting

Thomas. He recognized cunning when he came face to face with it, and from Ginger's long disappearance and her sudden flustered hurry, he had already decided to take a quick look through his suitcase. He knew how she felt about keeping his fraternity pin. "It won't take a minute, sir," he said, watching Ginger for any sign of apprehension.

She was bent over Shadow's collar, loosening it, and she didn't look up as she said, "Well, hurry. I'll meet you in the garage."

It would have been kind, he thought, hastily pawing through his own "unmentionables," if she had offered to accompany him to his underground hideaway and make sure he left nothing behind. She had done it for the rest of his family, running upstairs and down as if she couldn't bear to let them out of her sight. Yet she was abandoning him. Why? She, who never left him until the very last second, was sitting out in the car, sounding the horn.

"Hurry," she shouted, giving him barely enough time to stop in the kitchen and tell her parents good-by. And when he shoved her over and took the wheel, she said, "I'm not sure of the road that leads to the highway that leads to Dulles International Airport. It isn't far from here, but I don't know exactly how to get there."

"I do."

Spark Plug drove with the sureness that always made Ginger feel safe, and she leaned back. Then she sat up again to ask, "What's the matter? You look so—so grim. You aren't afraid of flying, are you?"

"Of course not." He smiled then, and though he didn't turn his head he said, "I just felt upset for a few minutes About leaving you to face this darned new school alone, I mean, and. . . ."

"And what?" she prompted, seeming all innocence.

"Nothing that I can do anything about right now. Something I'll have to work out when I get back to school."

"Oh." She leaned back again as if his answer satisfied her, and even moved nearer to him on the broad seat. "Spark Plug," she asked softly, "will you call me up, too? I'm not as brave about planes as you are, because I've only flown once when I was little, and I'll worry. But maybe," she amended hastily, "your mother could call back and tell me. It would be a lot cheaper."

"I'll phone you. And I'll do it once a week," he promised. "Which night would be best?"

"Oh, any," she answered, knowing he knew how dateless she would be. "Any school night would be fine because they're so boring, and sometimes I go out to dinner on week ends with Mom and Daddy."

"You'll be going to school affairs in no time," he told her, sure he spoke the truth and wishing he could be around to take her to them. "This little setback isn't going to wreck your year, and don't you let yourself think it is."

"I hope not."

They were approaching the big new airport; and while Spark Plug steered the car off the ramp and past a series of parking lots to the one near the Eastern Airlines office, she began to feel alone and lonely. And when she tagged along with him to have his ticket validated, she thought how handsome he looked in his lightweight sports jacket, with his dark hair neatly in place. He was a college student going off to some far place where she couldn't follow, to meet and talk with people she would never know, to live a daily life she couldn't visualize.

"Spark Plug," she asked, while they waited among a

crowd of passengers at a gate, "what does your fraternity house look like? Is it brick or wood, or what?"

"I'll send you a picture of it," he said. "And of the engineering buildings and the whole campus. I'll send you a bundle of post cards that will show you everything." He moved her away from the other people and bent his head to say, for her ears alone, "I'll mark my daily route on them, and you can know that I travel it every day with my little buddy trotting right along beside me."

"Ohhhh. . . ." The tears wouldn't stay back behind her eyes where they belonged, and in sudden compunction for what she had done, she clutched him and stammered, "I—I g-gave your pin back. I hid it in your suitcase. You won't hate me for it, will you?"

"I won't hate you," he said carefully, "because I understand why you did it, and you were right. Look here." He pulled back his jacket, and there was the little pin on his blue shirt, right where it belonged, over his heart. "I kept the handkerchief," he said, "just the way you kept mine. I guess they'll have to be enough for us for a while."

"Spark Plug Blake. . . ." The sight of the pin dried her tears. She felt outraged by his cupidity and the way he had left her to wonder if he knew, even letting her believe that he didn't. "I can't ever put anything over on you," she said with a groan. "It's—just—no—use—*trying!*"

"Then don't try any more. I was a little burned at first," he admitted, "because you hadn't talked the thing out, and then I understood why you couldn't. I'm such a determined cuss."

"That's why I like you."

The gates were open, and people began streaming past

them. Ginger, to her great surprise, found that she was clinging to him, and babbling, "Oh, dear. Oh, *deeear!* I wish—I wish. . . ."

"I'll have to go," Spark Plug said, interrupting her rush of words and bending to take her in his arms and kiss her. " 'By, little buddy."

"Good . . . by."

Ginger stood watching him hurry toward the plane, her nose pressed against the glass. He turned once as he went up the ramp, and waved, but she doubted if he could see the feeble return her hand gave.

Spark Plug was gone. He and his fraternity pin were going toward their special college world. She watched the plane taxi along the runway, turn and come past her again as it lifted its ponderous body from the ground. Then she went back to the parking lot and her car, and, through her tears, concentrated on the hazardous business of driving herself home.

"Well, Elston Howard Blake is high in the sky," she said to her parents, coming through the kitchen and finding them still on the porch.

"Was he sad about leaving?" her mother asked, watching Ginger drop the car keys on the table.

"I don't know. He walked right smartly out to the plane." Ginger stretched out on the chaise longue, and said, "But he did kiss me good-by."

"He did?" Both parents hoped she would volunteer more, and she didn't fail them.

"He almost had to," she said. "I was draped around his neck like an albatross. You see, I'd sneakily returned his fraternity pin, and was so conscience-stricken that I'd have taken it back if he'd offered it to me. I really believe I would have," she pondered aloud. "He's been so sweet all this week end—but then he always is—and I'm so scared of being alone and going to school."

"Oh, honey, you don't need to be," her father leaned forward to say. He had heard all about Miss Valerie De Camp while he and Spark Plug carpentered in the garage, so he said, as consolingly as he could, "Your mother and I were just talking about how hard everything seems to you now, but we're sure it will straighten out."

"That's what Spark Plug kept telling me. He's such an honest dope that he believes everyone is kindly underneath. He says if you just keep on digging out the kindness and don't give up, suddenly, *bam*, there it is, all exposed and beautiful."

"You've always believed that, too, dear," her mother said. "You've dug away at Patty for years."

"Yes, and she's still Patty."

"But you love her."

"Sure. And I love Spark Plug. You know," Ginger said, her voice changing to softness, "if I had a pair of wings right this minute, I'd buckle them on and fly out to Lafayette and meet his bus. I'd be there waiting for him."

"And would you fly back to us?" her father asked.

"I guess I'd have to." Ginger laughed then. "If I stayed I'd have to marry him, and we wouldn't have any money to live on. He blew his all the other night. Can't you just see us?" she sat up to say. "Me working somewhere—in a restaurant, maybe, although I'd be no help to the customers —and old Spark hunched over his books, not even looking up when I dragged in, tired, beat, and discouraged. Why,

I'd be worse off than a Fiji Islander on an iceberg. I guess a young marriage isn't for me."

"We're glad of that, honey."

"I want it beautiful," she went on dreamily, not hearing her father's words. "The wedding doesn't have to be big, just pretty and here on our lawn, with the groom, whoever he is, ready for whatever he plans to do and be. I'll help him, of course, if he needs it," she said, speaking her solemn thoughts aloud, "because I'll have a good education by then and won't have to take just any old job. I expect we'll have a pretty hard time at first, especially if my husband is young and just starting out, like Spark Plug."

She didn't see her parents glance at each other. The dusk was slowly deepening, and her father asked through it, "Do you think it will be Spark Plug?"

"Gracious, I don't know." Ginger came to with a start. "It will be, as of today," she said frankly, "but who knows about next year? Or five years from now when I finish college? I'm not quite seventeen, you know."

And this made her mother think it an appropriate time to relay a message. "Tim called while you were at the airport," she said.

"He did?" Ginger didn't see the glances that crossed again, a little relieved this time. If their dreamy daughter could jump up and become excited by the mere mention of a telephone call from another boy, she wasn't headed toward the altar. "What did he want?" she asked.

"He really wanted to talk to Spark Plug," her father told her, waiting for her to wilt. "Old Mr. Grimes lost his bowling ball, and he thought Spark Plug might have found it and put it away somewhere."

"Pooh. That was only camouflage," Ginger retorted, not in the least let down. "He was simply checking up on whether or not Spark Plug had left. Did he say he'd call back?"

"No, he said he was leaving for Penn State first thing in the morning."

"He'll call." Ginger turned on a small table lamp and asked, "Is anybody hungry? I am. I'll whip up a mess of all the leftovers we have." And on her way to the dark kitchen she stopped and said, "Isn't it crazy? Here I am with two suitors, both of them absent, and not a soul—either girl or boy—to brighten my days from here to yonder."

And having spoken so lightly, she felt her way to the sink. A flip of a switch would bring light into darkness. But why bother? she silently asked herself. Why be full of jokes and busy hustle when all she wanted to do was lie down on the polished floor like Sleeping Beauty, and stay in a coma for the whole nine months of school. What good was a buddy who was six hundred miles away, or even the absent Tim, whose deep, masculine voice could send prickles up and down her spine? "Oh, dear," she groaned, and switched on the light to keep from crying again.

CHAPTER SIX

GINGER walked self-consciously into the breakfast room the next morning wearing one of her new gray cotton skirts, her best white blouse, and carrying her blazer over her arm.

"I haven't any textbooks," she said, laying a worn leather-backed notebook and her fountain pen on the table. "Spark Plug and I were in such a tizzy Saturday after running into Valerie that I completely forgot them, and nothing was open on Sunday or Monday. It's a heck of a way to start out, isn't it?"

"Would you like me to pick you up after school?" her mother asked. "Then we can buy what you need."

"Oh, would you?" Ginger took a white purse and a brown one from the window sill and began transferring the contents of the white into the brown as she said, "If you wait right in front of the door I'll come flying out like the lady who was shot out of a cannon. That way, I won't have to linger about with my classmates."

"Wouldn't you rather take the car?"

"Nope, I'll ride the bus," she said. "I'll start out as one of many, and then follow along wherever they go. I won't be so conspicuous that way."

"Perhaps your big sister will meet you at the door," her father suggested, looking grim.

"Ha, ha, very funny." A horn blew a summons from the driveway, and as she picked up what little she had to take with her, she said, "Imagine me being called for in such style, right at my door. See you at three sharp, Mom."

The small bus was almost filled. One of the young assistant teachers was driving it, and when Ginger got on she stood up and looked back at her passengers. "Now, keep still, all of you," she ordered, "or I'll turn your names in to Mrs. Pierce." Then she looked at Ginger, and smiled. "It's always like this on our shakedown cruise. Good morning. I'm Miss Pettibone."

"Good morning," Ginger answered. "I suppose you already know that I'm Ginger Johnston. Do I take any special seat?"

"Just sit wherever you can stand the noise."

The door closed, the bus started off with grinding gears, and Ginger sat down beside a small girl who was making a face at a little boy behind her. Most of the children were young. Only three looked to be Dodie and Debbie's age, and four, three boys and a girl, might have been sophomores in high school. The rest were shedding their baby teeth. And all of them wore what they had worn all summer.

I suppose it's like not dressing for the first night on shipboard, Ginger thought, feeling conspicuous and wishing someone had told her that textbooks would be more important to buy than uniforms. All the children had books which they kept dropping, crayons which they kept spilling, paintboxes which clattered when they hit the floor; and they all knew each other. Ginger was grateful when the bus pulled in at a neighboring driveway and the Lawford girls got on. "Hi," she said, but they charged past her to their friends in the rear, so she sat silently beside the little girl, who continued making faces.

Nobody Ginger's age entered the bus; and when they reached the school she understood why. There were seventeen pupils in the senior class, and the other sixteen were stringing through the grove by the parking area. Juniors, seniors, in car pools or driving alone, were poking along, laughing, talking, and loaded down with books. All Ginger wanted to do was hop out of that bus and get inside before anyone saw her.

She charged through the square entrance hall that held no welcoming headmaster this morning, blundered along a corridor to find her home room where a round little man sat behind his desk in quiet meditation. "Good morning, sir," she tried to say brightly. "I'm a new student. I'm Virginia Johnston, but everyone calls me Ginger."

"Ah, Miss Johnston," he said formally, rising and making her a polite little bow that, with his guttural accent, identified him to her as a foreigner, probably German. "I am Doctor Liebermann, and my students address me as Herr Doktor. I think it started as a joke on me," he said, his eyes twinkling behind thick-lensed glasses, "but now I find it quite pleasant. You, in this school, will always be Miss Johnston."

"Oh," Ginger said inadequately, feeling as if she were being promoted to college age before her time.

"We believe in great courtesy here," he went on, staring at her, as if to impress both her and himself with the truth of his statement. "You are of adult age, yes?"

"Yes. I mean, no. I won't be seventeen for a week," she said. "I'm high school age."

"Ah, *zo*. But you are Miss Johnston, a young lady. The school finds it much prefer-able for its students to think of themselves as young ladies and young gentlemen, because it may inspire them to behave so. You will kindly take the third desk in the second row."

"Thank you, sir."

Ginger turned and looked at the room. It was so small that once it might have been a library when this was the manor house of the old estate, and the second row of desks was almost against the back wall. "I haven't bought my books, yet," she began to explain. "I'm terribly sorry, sir, but I haven't had time."

"Books you have not, but for learning you will always make time. Please remember that, Miss Johnston."

"Yes, sir. I will, and thank you, Herr Doktor."

Ginger walked to the third desk in the second row. It was a short walk, but it seemed miles because the stylish car-pool riders had begun filtering in. She sat down to watch them. There was the great Burke, she saw, giving the professor a hearty slap on the back that made the elderly man stiffen with resentment; there were Tina and Cecelia, walking with a bored slouch to their maple desks that were exactly like the one Ginger had had for years at home until her father had painted it white to match her sitting room. Both girls gave her a twitch of a smile that she tried to return with a broad one. A girl she didn't know sat primly down on her right, a homely, gangling boy gave her a nod as he slouched into the chair on her left, and Hal Friedendorfer scraped his chair unnecessarily as he took his seat in the front row. Two other boys, whose names she couldn't remember, gave Betsy a shove that knocked the whole front row of desks out of line.

Valerie—Ginger didn't recognize Valerie at first. Her hair was brown today. It hung in a long straight curtain on each side of her face and was parted by a narrow strip of bangs, so thick and long that it almost covered her eyes. Ginger, wondering how Valerie could see where she was going, was reminded of a sheep dog a neighbor back in Cheltham had owned. But Valerie could see quite well, apparently, for she flicked a wave in Ginger's direction and offered a "Hi, there."

"Hello," Ginger answered, aware that the Herr Doktor Liebermann would much prefer a proper "good morning."

He had moved out in front of his own desk now and was calling the class to order. "I wish to welcome you once again," he said in his stilted English. "It is good to return to work after a pleasant summer, yes?" Groans answered him, and he smiled. "It is, you will see," he went on. "Too much play makes for laziness. And also I want to make you acquainted with our new student, Miss Johnston. She will become Virginia to you, I am sure, although she has informed me that she prefers to be called Ginger. Class, you will please rise and introduce yourselves to Miss Johnston."

Ginger found herself shaking hands with students she had already met and ones she hadn't. Burke winked at her and audaciously caricatured the professor's formal little bow as he repeated his name, and Valerie, close behind him, said loudly for everyone to hear, "I'm Valerie De Camp, and I've been appointed to be your big sister."

"Yes, I know," Ginger couldn't resist saying. "You told me that Friday. Hello again, Valerie."

She tried to make some personal remark to the ones she knew ever so slightly, and to meet the new ones in a young, friendly way; and in a very few minutes it was over and they were back in their seats. Ginger looked at the two who had their desks on each side of hers. Elsie Semple, a homely girl with bad skin, fussed with her full pink skirt, and George Turnbull was sprawled in his chair with his feet in the narrow aisle. Elsie looked like a good student, while George—she was sure that George was the kind who would slide his chair closer to hers so he could copy from her examination paper. But perhaps he wouldn't be taking German, she thought hopefully. This was the seniors' home room, so it didn't necessarily mean that seventeen seniors would meet here very often or that George would sit beside her in other classes.

She was glad she had added elementary German to her advanced French, because she liked the Herr Doktor. Her schedule was heavy, but—and she shrugged without knowing it—what else had she to do except study?

A bell rang and, copying Elsie, she put her purse in the bottom left-hand drawer of her desk and prepared to rise. But Bernadine MacKensey was passing out typed slips of paper. These were the luncheon menus.

Veal and macaroni or a ham sandwich with potato salad. Ginger chose the sandwich and salad. Tea, coffee, milk. She checked milk and hesitated between Jell-O and ice cream. Neither one appealed to her at that hour in the morning, but she marked the Jell-O. Then she filed out with the rest of the class, leaving her luncheon list on

Dr. Liebermann's desk as the others did. Where was the physics lab? she wondered.

Some students turned one way along the corridor, some the other, and her big sister Valerie went off with Burke and a few of her faithful followers. Ginger decided to ask a group that had stopped to compare schedules.

"I don't know where to go," she said, going over to them. "I know I'm due at Physics I, but I don't remember having seen the room."

"Oh. Well. . . ." One of the girls who had been friendly during the introductions looked at the card Ginger held out. "I'm going there," she said.

"May I walk along with you?" Ginger asked, grateful to have found a guide.

"Sure. See you in history, gang." And they started off together.

The girl, Ginger remembered, was Mittie Marsten. She was cute, with a brown pony tail and big blue eyes; and walking beside her through the glass-walled corridor that led to the laboratory, Ginger said, as a compliment: "Not many girls could wear their hair pulled back the way you do. I tried it once and I looked like the dickens."

"Thanks." Mittie smiled but seemed embarrassed. "Here's the lab," she said, opening the door to a room where two-thirds of the senior class was assembled. "Just take a seat at either table."

Ginger stopped and looked around. Only two chairs were vacant. One was beside George, the other beside the pimply Elsie. She chose Elsie in a rush, and it wasn't until she was seated that she saw Burke on her other side, with Valerie just beyond him. She tried to rise then, and flee to the other table but it was too late. Mittie was already there, and Burke was saying, "I saved this seat for you."

"Thank you."

Last year, she would have tossed back, "I'll bet you did." Now she tried not to mind the furtive, amused looks that were passing around. There was nothing she could do, so she sat taking notes on tomorrow's assignment, writing down the numbers of the pages she would have to study when she had her book. And when Burke offered to share his with her, she shook her head without answering. It was the longest hour she had ever sat through; and when it finally ended, she hustled along the hallways, praying she could find her own way to her next class in a hurry.

At lunchtime she followed the crowd to the dining room and was given a tray with a card on it that said, *Miss V. Johnston.* Where to go now? No table had been assigned to her, so she sat down at the first one she came to. It, unfortunately, had always been considered the special table of a group of ardent art students; and unloading her tray, she was unaware that she had usurped someone's chair and that a girl glared at her before she flounced off to sit somewhere else. She did learn, however, from the conversation that was passed back and forth, that certain tables were staked out by certain groups and it was a shame that Lois Jean couldn't sit at this one. By then it was too late to change, so she left the Jell-O she didn't want anyway, excused herself, and went out to the registrar's office, where a kindly secretary showed her a chart of the different buildings and told her where to find her classrooms. And finally, after no more mishaps, after wary peeks at chairs or desks, she finished her last class.

"Thank goodness, you're here!" she cried to her mother, flinging herself into the car as she had said she would. "This day has been *awful!* It was even worse than I thought it would be."

"What happened, honey?" her mother asked, as they drove away. "Was Valerie. . . ."

"It wasn't only Valerie," Ginger interrupted miserably. "It was the whole school. Or perhaps it was me. I've gotten to the point where I think it was—me, I mean."

"Why dear?"

"I couldn't make friends with anybody. I tried. But I just couldn't, that's all. Nobody liked me."

"Oh, child, that's foolish." Mrs. Johnston was sure Ginger was either exaggerating or that she had been too shy in a new school. "Your classmates have always liked you," she said. "Why, back in Cheltham. . . ."

"Maybe that was habit," Ginger broke in. "I always pased from grade to grade with the same kids, so how do I know if they liked me or not? When I reached high school I was still one of a bunch."

"But Patty, Mary Lou, Tim, Spark Plug, Steve Harding, and dozens of others I could name did. They weren't *all* in your class, dear, yet they liked you."

But Ginger wasn't listening. "I don't think we were rude or clannish," she was saying, sitting bunched up with her head bent. "I remember when I was in the fifth grade and a new little girl moved in from the country and came to our school. She had on a funny-looking pink silk dress and could have been an awful crumb for all we knew, but all the girls fought to sit in her seat with her and show her what we were studying. She chose me the first morning, and Patty wouldn't speak to me all day. I don't think I look any worse than that kid did, so how could a whole school make fun of me?"

"Oh, Ginger, they didn't do *that!*" her mother cried, aghast.

"I think they did," Ginger said carefully, lacing her hands in her lap and studying each finger as it slid into place. "My class did, at least. I only tangled with some juniors once, at lunch, when I sat where I didn't belong. They let me know it. There must be something about me that doesn't fit in at Paxton Hill. I wish I knew what it is."

"Are the ones in your class friendly with each other?" her mother asked.

"I guess so. Certain ones walk to classes together and scramble for seats next to each other. A girl named Margo Lewis walked back to my home room with me this afternoon, but I'm sure it was an accident because she kept a step ahead of me all the way."

"And Valerie?"

"Mom, it doesn't do any good to try and blame what happened to me on Valerie." Ginger sat up and said, "I did that, at first, because I'd goofed the other day."

"No, you didn't, Ginger."

"Well, Valerie thought I did. She can be snooty to me, and maybe her special group can follow along, but gosh, she can't make a whole class brush me off. She just can't, Mom, so I wish I knew what's so wrong."

"Ginger Johnston, stop talking that way," her mother admonished. "There's nothing wrong with you, and you know it. Now, tell me about the whole day and let me see if I can put my finger on anything that might help you."

"Okay." Ginger began wth her bus ride and was telling about rushing inside the school to avoid the others who had driven up in cars when her mother interrupted her.

"Perhaps you should have taken the Sprite," she said. "Daddy can ride with Mr. Elkins three days a week, and I can give you the station wagon on the other two."

But Ginger shook her head. "The bus suits me fine," she declared, "and it's the sensible way for me to go. I wouldn't like driving all that way alone just to impress a bunch of kids who couldn't care less about how I got there."

"Oh, dear. Go on."

So Ginger told about finding her home room and meeting Herr Doktor Liebermann. She became quite engrossed with that part of her tale, but finally she said, "He's a darling and I really enjoyed my German class with him." And then she went on to relate the fiasco of her physics class.

"Oh, Ginger," her mother said, "didn't you really see Burke when you chose that place at the table?"

"Of course I didn't." Ginger was indignant. "Don't tell me that you think I did it on purpose," she said, startled. "If you'd had to go through what I have with Valerie, you wouldn't take a chance on being anywhere near him. Why, once he even leaned over my notebook and said, 'You're putting down the wrong page.' Then he actually took my pen and wrote *WE 8-2669*. And I'm sure I felt his foot press against mine, and not accidentally, either. He's slimy and sly, and if he's the only one at Paxton Hill who can like me, I don't want to be liked."

"Oh, dear," was all her mother could say.

"I guess that was the worst hour of the day," Ginger went on more calmly. "I did sit at the wrong table during lunch, but I left as soon as I could and I walked to classes by myself. I—well, I didn't bother anybody again. I suppose that's something in my favor."

"Honey, listen to me." Mrs. Johnston had to back the car in to a vacant space before a bookstore and park it beside a meter before she could turn off her motor and say, "I know you're not to blame for whatever has gone wrong at this school. I know that as surely as I'm sitting here. But what to do about it is another matter."

"There isn't anything to do," Ginger said flatly. "The best way is to let it die on the vine. Come on. You can put a nickel in the meter while I go in and start buying my books."

Her father was home when they came up from the garage. He was pouring himself a glass of iced tea in the kitchen, and when Ginger said, "Hi, Daddy," and went on through to the front hall with her books he asked his wife anxiously, "How did her day go?"

"It was terrible." Mrs. Johnston sat down on the kitchen stool and shook her head as she asked, "What are we going to do, Stuart? The whole class behaved wretchedly today, and Ginger has the idea that she's the one who is wrong, not the school. What have we done to our child?"

"I wish I knew." He dragged in a chair from the breakfast room, one of the old-fashioned soda-fountain chairs that the three Johnstons had thought so quaint, and sat down astride it, "One thing is certain," he said, resting his arms on its wire back and watching his tea swirl around the ice, "if Ginger isn't happy in that school we'll have to get her out of there and send her back where she belongs."

"Oh, Stuart, we can't," she answered, closing her eyes

against what she knew Ginger would say to such a suggestion, then opening them again to explain, "Ginger's like you. She's a fighter. She won't ever turn back. I feel it—I know it. She would rather the whole school would hate her than be a coward."

"Then what's left to do?"

"I don't know a quick answer to that. This is something I can't imagine happening to Ginger."

"Do we let her go off to college with a complex?" he persisted. "She's quite apt to get one, you know. Kids do. They crawl into a shell and let the good things in life pass them by."

"I'm sure Ginger won't."

"But what's the solution? Are we supposed to sit in our fine fancy house and buy her a car, like a lollipop, and then let the chips fall where they may? Un-huh. Ginger's our daughter and we love her. We've spent seventeen years watching her grow up beautifully, so we aren't going to let her get frostbitten like a last-year's rose bush that you can dig up and throw away. I'll bet a dollar to a doughnut that our child's upstairs crying her heart out. Do you think I'm going to sit here drinking iced tea and let her take the brunt of a selfish move I made? We'll move back to Cheltham."

"Stuart, we can't." Katherine Johnston went over to put her arms around him and say, "It was a bad day, I'll admit, but it and all the others to follow can't break Ginger. We've taught her to be strong and sturdy. If she isn't, then we've wasted seventeen years of love and training. Let's give her a chance to prove herself, dear. I'm sure she can, and will."

He was unconvinced, but he nodded. "She's just a little

girl," he said with a sigh. "A few years ago she was wearing a sun suit, and now she's wearing the uniform of that dad-blasted school. I can't see it, kitten. I just can't see it."

"Can't see what?" Ginger asked, standing in the hall door.

She wore red shorts and a faded yellow shirt, and she scolded, " Why are you two sitting here in the dark? Doesn't anybody ever think of starting dinner unless I'm around to remind you?"

"We were just about to do it, dear," her mother answered, while her father stared at her in a numb, wretched way.

"Then let's do it." She came across the kitchen and patted the top of her father's head as she passed him. "It's nice to have you home, Mr. J," she said. "But let me tell you something. If you're looking glum because of me, you don't need to." And she added in a loud whisper, "Mom's a worry bird."

CHAPTER SEVEN

GINGER'S second day of school was much like her first except that nine-tenths of the students were in uniform, regular seats were assigned in the different classes, and the Lawford girls discovered her on the bus and proudly escorted her to their table in the dining room, where she ate with a group of seventh and eighth graders. She was still an outcast, the rejected lamb in a flock of seventeen sheep, and although she accepted it, she still wondered why it had to be.

And then, at the end of Friday afternoon, Valerie unexpectedly remembered her big-sister duties and stopped beside Ginger's desk in their home room to say, "There's a meeting of the seniors in here after school, to elect officers and the chairman of the committees, you know."

"Yes, I read it on the bulletin board," Ginger answered, having learned to take care of herself.

"Have you a way to get home?"

"Umhum." Ginger had arranged for that, but why tell Valerie that her mother was coming for her? If the whole class could behave like a bunch of cold fish, she could be as icy as something straight out of a freezer. She almost smiled at the thought which was simply a carry-over from her last hour's enjoyable class in metaphors and similes, but decided that the unaccustomed expression might stretch her face out of shape. So she stacked the books she would need, reached down to the bottom drawer for her purse, and said, "Thanks."

"For what?" Valerie asked, peeking out from under her bang. "I was trying to be nice and you brushed me off."

"Oh, excuse me." Ginger sat up, all attention, and a smile actually did break through, briefly, before she said, "I appreciate it. Is there anyone special you want me to vote for?"

"Well. . . ." Valerie was caught off guard. Ginger wasn't supposed to know that her big sister was recruiting votes, finishing up the politicking that had been going on all week, but she appeared to. "Just—just use your own judgment," she stammered, backing away. "I guess you've had time to learn who's best qualified to be class president."

"I think so." Ginger leaned back in her chair, trying to look like a member of an election board evaluating the party's candidates, or a judge on the bench, or a desk sergeant in a police court. She only looked what she was, a tired, unhappy schoolgirl who dreaded the next hour.

But Valerie failed to see it. She was watching Dr. Liebermann leave and the favored few crowd around Ted Haines, who had been last year's president. "Be seeing you," she said to Ginger, and hurried to the front of the room to learn what was going on.

Ginger stayed where she was, hands folded on her desk as if she were in class, and watching the proceedings that were, to say the least, informal. Some students sat on desks, and those who belonged behind them pulled their chairs out in the aisles so they could see. The back row, with Ginger in it, was deserted.

"Look, kids," Ted said above the noise, "we've got to elect a new class president. I'm due at football practice in fifteen minutes, so does anybody want to nominate some guy to take over for me?"

"I nominate Burke Mathews," Valerie said promptly, having already learned that she couldn't win. "George, you second it."

"I second it," George boomed out dutifully. And he added, "All in favor say 'aye.' "

A chorous of ayes rang out, and no one noticed that Ginger was silent.

Burke was duly elected president, and Ted said, "Thanks, pal," before he loped out.

The vice-presidency, Ginger was sure, would go to Valerie, and she was surprised when it didn't. "I'd rather be treasurer," Valerie said, standing up to face them when her name was proposed. "That way, I could be head of the Pep Club, and could organize the dances and things. Somebody has to go out and dig up the money," she went on hastily, when Cecelia looked cross, "and I know most of the parents around here. The dance committee fell apart last year, and you all know it." Betsy, who had been the junior vice-president of the club, looked abashed, but Valerie showed her no mercy. "The dances and trips to the games were lousy," she said, "simply because we couldn't get people interested enough to go. I'd rather have the Pep Club than any other job."

She also became—after a dull boy had found himself

with the useless job of vice-president and Betsy's wounds were healed by being made secretary—assistant editor of the weekly newspaper and the yearbook, with Burke as editor in chief. She was also the girls' head cheerleader, with Burke calling the cheers.

Ginger wondered why she had been given a special invitation to stay, because the whole affair had been carefully planned in advance. A few looked unhappy with the results, but when Valerie stood in front of them and said kindly, "I'm going to make each of you the head of some committee," they brightened a little. "You'll have to appoint juniors to be your assistants," she went on importantly. "And since they're a pretty stupid bunch you'll have your hands full."

Shouts and boos greeted her remark, and she actually looked embarrassed as she said quickly, "Sorry. I forgot that we were juniors last year. But we were *smart* juniors," she added, to draw them back to her.

"I wasn't," Betsy spoke up. "I was the junior vice-president of the Pep Club, remember? And you just said I did a lousy job."

"Oh, well, it was the seniors' fault." Valerie walked over to put her arm around Betsy, and told the whole class, "I was on one of Betsy's committees, and we were in a bind. We couldn't organize anything on our own. Betsy knows it as well as I do."

Ginger snatched the opportunity to slip out. She wasn't needed here. She had no idea of what committees Valerie would organize, but knew she wouldn't be asked to head one. She and the vice-president, who was sitting lonesomely to one side and listening to Burke proclaim that this would be the best class Paxton Hill had ever turned out, wouldn't be missed if they left and never came back. So she picked up her books and edged around the outside of the room to the door.

"Good-by, dear alma mater, until I see you for another long week," she mumbled, walking purposefully along the empty corridor as if she didn't give a whoop. Then she heard padding footsteps behind her.

It was Burke; and he called, "Hey, wait. The meeting isn't over yet."

"For me, it is." Ginger turned her head but didn't stop. "We elected officers," she said, "so what else is there to do?"

"Why, gosh," he said, "I need an art editor and a story editor for the yearbook and the newspaper."

"You can appoint them," she said with a shrug. "Not today, because the teachers will have a say in it, but when it's all worked out. The ones who've been on the staff will simply move up to higher positions, heads of the different departments."

"You seem to know a lot about it."

"I do." She was at the door now and she turned to face him. "I was assistant editor for my high school last year and was elected to be editor this year. We had over a thousand students, so we had to work like fury for the job." Then she went out and down the steps.

"Ginger, wait." Burke leaped down after her and caught her arm. "I think you're getting a raw deal here," he said, "and I've thought so ever since you came. I couldn't help that phony election today, and, frankly, I didn't want to. I've worked hard, too, for what I'm getting, and I've got a father who'd clobber me if I didn't make good and come out on top."

"Then I'm glad you've made it."

"But I'll need help on this newspaper business because I don't know too much about it. I wrote some pieces last year but I wasn't on the staff, so won't you help me? Please?" he begged.

"No." Ginger shook her head. She could see her mother sitting in the car, pretending to read a book while she covertly watched the two by the steps. "I'm in enough trouble with this school as it is," she said, "and it all started because you were too nice to me the first day I came. Perhaps I was fresh at first, but I didn't mean to be. I'd never been in a private school before, so I'm sure I went at it too hard and was overfriendly." She sighed, then said, "Thanks, Burke, for asking me to help in the editing department, but I can't do it. You'd better go back." And she walked on out to the car.

"Who was that boy you were talking to?" her mother asked, laying aside her book and starting the motor.

"Now, who do you think?" Ginger slammed the door and asked in her turn, "Who would be stupid enough, and determined enough, to follow me out here? The great senior class president, Burke Mathews, that's who," she said, without waiting for her mother to guess. "You know," she went on, grim-lipped, plopping her own books down on the seat, "I think he's using me as a weapon against Valerie, and not a secret weapon, either. I may be unfair to him, but I have a hunch that he's playing me against her to make her jealous and keep her in line."

"But, honey, Valerie knows. . . ."

"Valerie doesn't know anything," Ginger broke in. "She's the dumbest, the silliest, the most obviously stupid girl I've ever met, yet she's got the whole school thinking she's wonderfully cute, witty, and wise. Let's not talk about the school, I'm fed to the teeth with it."

"All right." Mrs. Johnston stifled her curiosity about the election and said, "From now on we'll talk about the long telephone chat I had with Spark Plug's mother. She said they're having a party tomorrow night and she can't find the recipe I gave her for my shrimp casserole. She said everything's fine, and Spark Plug plans to call you Sunday."

And so it went while September dwindled into October. Ginger had a birthday, and as the trees let go of their bright, beautiful leaves, she continued to wonder how anyone who wasn't actually behind bars could still be in prison. She had a beautiful house to wander about in, a yard to rake for lack of something better to do, yet she was as confined as any parolee who was sent out to work every day, then returned to his jail at night.

Laurel Hills still provided no teen-agers, or if it did, she didn't see them. Bud Traymore still had his job after school and his steady girl; Peggy Seaton went to a school in Washington and stayed for the extracurricular activities so she could drive home with her father, then either went dashing off on dates or spent her evenings on the telephone. Ginger often wondered how Peggy could make so many college dances on week ends. The Smiths, being Army, had been transferred to Spain, so their house was for sale and the twins stayed on with their grandmother. Laurel Hills, Ginger constantly told her rake, was a lonely, loney place for a girl her age.

Even the month of October let her down because it gave her fewer and fewer leaves to rake, and anyway her father liked to put on his country clothes and tussle with them. He said raking made him feel like a property owner and provided a better family day on Saturday than a golf game. But he could go off and play golf whenever he wanted to, Ginger told herself, and her mother could play bridge. Together, Mr. and Mrs. Johnston had endless evenings with friends. Even Shadow had found a pal, a German shepherd that was allowed to roam through the woods and was a good rabbit chaser. Ginger was the only Johnston who had nothing to do but study.

"I don't like it," her father said one evening, sitting in the living room and watching Ginger in the library, looking up something in the encyclopedia. "What are we going to do?"

"Do you think it would help if I talked to one of her teachers? The headmaster, perhaps?"

"I don't think he knows Ginger's alive."

They both listened to feet dragging lonesomely up the stairs, and Mrs. Johnston said, "I'm going to do it."

"What will you say?"

"Heavens, I don't know. I'm simply going to tell him, I suppose, that our daughter is being discriminated against, and ask him why."

"Will he care?"

"I'm not sure, but I'm going to try it."

"And if he ignores you?"

"We'll try something else."

It was easy to say but hard to do. Mrs. Johnston watched Ginger start off on the bus the next morning, and then, as an old saying goes, she "girded her loins." That simply meant that she put on her new knitted navy-blue suit, blue suede gloves and blue shoes, and stuffed her wallet and driving credentials into a navy-blue purse. Then she drove purposefully to the main door of Paxton Hill, ignored a sign which read NO PARKING, and was ushered in to the headmaster's plush office, where she seated herself in a leather chair, much too large for her, and waited for the patriarch of the institution to come back from wherever he was. It even meant that she held on to her courage.

Ginger was her dearly loved child, she kept telling herself. Ginger's parents had got her into this mess, so it was up to them, to one of them, at least, to get her out. She sat and waited.

"Ah, Mrs. Johnston," Dr. Cartwright said pleasantly, having been briefed about his visitor and assuming Ginger to be as happy as a cricket on a fireplace hearth, "it's nice to see you. What can we do for you?"

Katherine Johnston wasted no time in telling him. She tried not to be emotional, but it was hard to keep her voice steady as she said, "I came because Ginger isn't happy in her school, Dr. Cartwright. She always has been before, so it's a shock to her father and me to learn that she feels quite alone in this one. It may be Ginger's fault," she leaned forward to say, "although she's never had trouble before. I want very much to learn what is wrong."

She stopped because there was nothing more she could explain until he spoke in his turn, and she watched him thoughtfully rub a finger back and forth across his narrow mustache. But at last he said, "This comes as a great surprise to me. I've always considered Miss Johnston—Ginger,

I should say—to be very well adjusted. She always smiles and speaks so pleasantly, but of course I see very little of the students. Suppose we ask my assistant, Mrs. Pierce, to come in. She knows your daughter far better than I do."

"Thank you."

Katherine Johnston watched him flip a switch on a small box on his desk, then lean toward it and speak. She had met Mrs. Pierce when Ginger had come for her interview, and had liked her. So when a tall thin woman with a narrow face and perfectly waved gray hair came in, she gave a smile of relief. Mrs. Pierce looked as if she might know exactly where the trouble lay.

"I'm sorry Ginger isn't happy here," Mrs. Pierce said, when the situation had been explained to her, and she pulled another leather chair closer to the desk. "Frankly, I've noticed it and been troubled about it. So have her teachers, especially Dr. Liebermann. All the teachers," she said earnestly, "like Ginger very much and think she's outstanding."

"I'm glad." Katherine Johnston slid forward, then sat back, trying so hard to look relaxed and not like a fluttery mother that she almost missed what Mrs. Pierce was saying.

"Young people can be very thoughtless and cruel," the headmistress pointed out carefully, defending both sides in this sad affair. "Our seniors have gone through high school together and so are a small, clannish group. It isn't like a big class where there are many cliques." She stopped and said after a sigh, "We seem to have just one here."

"Yes, I know." Mrs. Johnston felt they understood each other, so she asked, "Do you think Ginger did anything that would keep her out of that clique?"

"No, definitely not. Or if she did, it was inadvertent and misunderstood." Mrs. Pierce looked over at Dr. Cartwright, who was shuffling papers about, quite lost and useless to their conversation, and said gently, "Stephen, suppose you go out and talk to the carpenter for me. Mrs. Johnston and I can manage quite well without you."

"Thank you, Mary." He was grateful to be released, so he shook hands with Mrs. Johnston in a pleasant, hurried way and made a thankful escape.

"Now," Mary Pierce said when they were alone, "about the freeze treatment Ginger is getting. Please don't think we haven't noticed, Mrs. Johnston, because we have. Dr. Liebermann first brought it to our attention, and we held a faculty meeting and talked to different members of the class. But there is very little we can do when faced with a blanket denial of any intentional slight."

"I see." Katherine Johnston looked down at her blue purse and massaged its soft leather as she said, "I suppose I see, even though I don't want to. What you're telling me is that it will never be any different, that you as a school are powerless to make seventeen teen-agers get along together, and that we should move Ginger somewhere else."

"Oh, not at all." Mrs. Pierce leaned forward to say with deep feeling, "I'm simply trying to explain a situation to you and hoping we can go on to a solution of it. We don't want to lose Ginger. We'll do everything in our power to keep her and make her happy with us. I think our first step is patience."

"We, her father and I, have tried to be patient." Mrs. Johnston hated to say it but she had to. "We've spent almost six weeks being patient and telling Ginger to be. She was, at first; then she began to feel that something was wrong with her. It's very hard to see your child lose confidence in herself."

"Oh, I know it is, and Ginger must never do that. So please let me work something out. Suppose we choose her for the lead in the class play or urge her to go out for the girls' basketball team? Anything that will start her mingling with the school."

Mrs. Johnston found herself giving an amused smile. "You'd lose every game," she said, "with Ginger on the court, and she isn't an actress. It wouldn't work, Mrs. Pierce. She'd have more enemies than she has now."

"Then let me try something else," Mrs. Pierce pleaded. "We can't lose Ginger. She's such a credit to the school, personally as well as scholastically. Let me explain matters to just the officers of the senior class and tell them it's their problem, one they've created. Teen-agers are really very understanding, once a situation is carefully explained to them," she said, wishing she could punish them as they deserved. "Let me talk to Burke Mathews, the president. He's a fine boy and may come up with an answer."

"Oh, mercy, no!" Mrs. Johnston jumped up and her purse fell off her lap. She hadn't intended to stand so soon, but since she was up she retrieved her purse. Nothing had been gained by the talk, but she said: "Thank you for listening to me, anyway. I suppose you must listen to a lot of parents with grievances."

"But not like yours. You have a legitimate grievance Mrs. Johnston, and it reflects on our school. Believe me when I say that I'm going to do everything in my power to rectify it."

"Thank you."

Katherine Johnston walked to the door, no better off than when she had come; and following her, Mary Pierce was already wondering what punishment she could inflict on Valerie De Camp that would whip her into line.

CHAPTER EIGHT

"I CAN'T bear to watch Ginger getting thinner and thinner," Stuart Johnston said to his wife, sitting in the living room and listening to Ginger talking in monosyllables with Patty on the telephone in the library. "Heaven knows, she hadn't a spare pound to lose, and now she's positively scrawny."

"What are we going to do about it? We tried, and nothing happened."

"Move her. Find another school."

Mrs. Johnston laid down her magazine and looked at him. "Haven't we tried that, too?" she asked. "We talked about the new high school that's finally finished, and you suggested driving her down to Lilac Road where she can catch the bus, and even offered to buy her a car. And what did she say?"

"She said she had started at Paxton Hill," he answered uncomfortably, "and there she would stay. She said the courses are tops and she intends to stick it out. That's what she said."

"And that's what she'll do. As I've said before, Stuart," Mrs. Johnston pointed out, "our daughter has a lot of your tenacity. She knows what she wants and nothing can stop her from going after it."

"How about telling her to ask Patty down for the week end?"

"Tim's coming to take her to the VMI football game in Lexington."

"She doesn't sound overjoyed about it, if you ask me." Stuart Johnston had heard the dull side of Ginger's conversation, and in his frustration he gave his newspaper a flap, much as if he were slapping at a troublesome fly. And when Ginger came out of the library and turned toward the stairway, he called, "What did Patty want?"

"Nothing." Ginger paused with her foot on the bottom step. "Just to tell me about her new formal," she said. "It's blue, and it has yards and yards of some new gauzy fabric in the skirt, and she looks divine in it. It brings out the blue in her eyes. Anything else you want to know?"

"Yes." Her father was suddenly angry. Not at Ginger, but at the whole youthful world that could have happy, cherished memories of its high school years. "Come here, honey," he said, trying to sound calm. And when Ginger obediently stood in the archway, he asked, "Don't you want a new dress? If you're going down to this football shindig, maybe you should have one."

"It isn't that kind of a day, Daddy," Ginger said. "I have my three-piece suit, and anyway, I may not go."

"Why not?"

Ginger swallowed several times, then clapped her hand over her mouth. "I'm sorry, Daddy," she said, "but—oh, gosh, I think I'm going to be sick."

This was the first intimation the Johnstons had had

that Ginger was suffering from nausea and stomach pains. Every day, she now admitted under pressure, the pains plagued her. For the last two weeks she had become an almost permanent resident of the girls' rest room, where she first lost what little she had eaten, then gagged and clutched at the fiery pain in her stomach.

A doctor was called; a specialist was consulted; X rays were taken. Ginger was put on a fatty diet that nauseated her even more; and when Friday evening came and brought Tim with it, she was lying in a hospital bed, looking as white as the spread that covered her.

Tim tiptoed cautiously in, escorted as far as the door by a student nurse who looked about to swoon from love at first sight, and Ginger hunched herself higher on her pillows and grinned at him.

"Hi," she said. "Park your box of flowers and your pussy-cat grin somewhere and come over here so I can tell you how like a stinker I feel."

"Think nothing of it, Ginger-cookie." Tim laid his box across a lap that made no more than a tiny mound under the covers, and said, "You poor kid."

He looked so handsome standing beside her. He was the handsomest and dearest person she had seen since school had started. He looked like someone straight out of a movie; and memorizing his smooth brown hair, his brown eyes, and pointed chin for future pleasure, she said, "Oh, gosh, I'm glad to see you."

"You don't look sick." He, in turn, studied her feathery curls that had behaved nobly during a bout of fever, her pale cheeks that reflected a little glow from the fluffy pink bed jacket her mother had rushed out to buy, and said, "You look really pretty."

"I'll bet," Ginger retorted, trying to sound gay as she began untying a green ribbon on the box. The stubborn knot resisted her weak fingers, so she pushed the box aside and said, "I'm so sorry I can't go to the game with you."

"What game? Now, you don't think for one minute that I'm going to leave my comfortable pad with your folks, do you? Give up a week end in a real home? No, sir. Timmy boy stays right here."

"You're only doing it for me," Ginger answered with a sigh, not looking as happy as he had thought she would. "It'll be lonesome for you, because I can't go home until Sunday."

"And I'll be the fellow with the white convertible who will call for you and carry you out. We can listen to the game on the radio tomorrow afternoon and play ticktacktoe in the evening. I only have one class on Monday, so I'm taking a cut in it, and we can lounge around your house until I have to leave. What's an ulcer between friends?"

"It's only a *little* ulcer," Ginger said, feeling better, and stronger, and happier than she had in weeks. So strong, in fact, that the lid of the box slid off easily and she cradled a mass of pink roses against her cheek. "Who would ever think of me getting an ulcer?" she said, smiling at him above the flowers. "Isn't it a silly thing to have, at my age?"

"No."

Tim was surprisingly serious. He and Ginger's parents had had a long talk when, in spite of Ginger's embarrassed telephone call about having to cancel the trip to Lexington, he had come racing up their driveway just as they finished dinner.

"What gives with Ginger-cookie?" he had asked, sitting

down at the dining-room table and eating what was left of a small meat loaf and vegetables. "What's she doing in a hospital?"

Then they told him. Ginger, they took turns saying, had been nervous and worried about her rejection by the school, but neither of them had realized how much it troubled her. They had noticed her loss of appetite, but since she never mentioned the pain she suffered after she ate and they didn't know how much bicarbonate of soda she took, they had thought she would pick up again when things at school straightened out. By nature, Ginger was a happy extrovert, so—an ulcer? Never once had they thought of an ulcer, not even when she was put in the hospital. Appendicitis, nervous indigestion, yes, but never an ulcer. It had surprised them to learn that ulcers aren't confined to adults: babies often develop them from insecurity. Ginger's, fortunately, was caught at an early stage, and she had a competent specialist.

"I'll tell you a little story, Ginger-cookie," he said now, smoothing back her hair and laying his cheek beside hers on the pillow as only Tim could do without making her uncomfortably aware of his nearness. "It's about a little girl who moved from a small town to a big, rich community. She was a dear, trusting little girl, and she had never, never run afoul of the evil machinations of her sex."

"I didn't run afoul of them," Ginger said, chuckling. "Let's face it. I didn't know straight up from nothing."

"All right, so the dear little girl didn't know. She thought the whole blamed world was made up of sweetness and spun-sugar candy." Tim's hand, reaching for hers, was pricked by a thorn deceptively hidden in the green leaves of the roses, and he sat up to say, "Ouch." Then he showed her his finger from which a drop of blood oozed. "That's what happened to the little girl," he told her. "How better can I prove my point? That's the poor, trusting, bleeding, ulcerous little girl."

They were laughing together when a nurse came in to say that visiting hours were over. Ginger had shown him the box of school stationery Dr. Cartright had sent on behalf of the school, the handkerchief from Mrs. Pierce, the ornate get-well card from dear Herr Doktor Liebermann, the fancy florist card that was all she had left of the carnations her class had sent. The carnations had been unhappy in the hospital atmosphere and had wilted the next day, but she had kept their attached card, hoping it really meant a change in the viewpoint of the seniors.

And on Sunday, Tim came alone to take her home.

Her father had arranged for her release, but it was Tim who hooked his arm through hers and guided her hesitant footsteps. "Come on now, Ginger-cookie," he urged when they reached the car and she seemed reluctant to go back to the world she had left. "What are you stalling for?"

"I don't know." She watched him put her suitcase on the back seat and said thoughtfully, "I don't want to go back to school, I guess. It was nice in this safe, sterile place."

"But is isn't your life. And you don't have to go back to school for a while, if ever."

"I'll go back on Tuesday, after you've left." Her chin lifted, and she sat down on the bright red leather, watching him close the door. "Last summer," she said, when he was beside her, "Daddy told me that I'm growing, building, whatever you want to call it. It's darned hard."

Tim started the motor and drove for several blocks before he said, "I don't know how to advise you, Ginger-cookie. Being me, I suppose I'd say, 'Oh, nuts to the whole business,' and quit. I like to have fun wherever I am." And he suddenly asked, "Have you talked to Spark Plug about this and asked his advice?"

"Why should I?" Ginger leaned back and shook her head. "Why should I?" she asked again, closing her eyes. "There's really nothing for anyone to advise me about. I'm me, and I have to live the life I have. I fluffed out, so that's that. Spark Plug wouldn't understand such weakness. You do. You came anyway after I'd let you down, and that's enough for me. Let's not talk about Spark Plug."

"It suits me fine."

Tim drove the short distance home. Parking in the driveway, he again became the custodian of Ginger's suitcase because her mother and father came rushing out to the car; and without waiting to watch the glad reunion, he went upstairs and set the small bag in Ginger's room.

It was a pretty room, he thought, looking about, then going on to her sitting room beyond. Here was a place of dreams, a young girl's dreams. Both Ginger's present and her past were here. The present was in her schoolbooks neatly stacked on the desk and a copy of *The Rise and Fall of the Third Reich* still open where she had left it. The past was a desk set she had won as a literary prize when she was a sophomore, the silly stuffed donkey he had bought her at the country fair last year. The donkey sat in a pink chair, and beside it was the rickety magazine rack that Spark Plug had made in manual training years ago. Party favors and keepsakes were carefully preserved under the glass top of a coffee table; and bending over to see if any gift of his was there, he remembered that Spark Plug had made the table for Ginger when she learned she would have to move. Dear little Ginger-cookie, he thought, giving the donkey a pat before he went back downstairs.

Ginger was resting on the long sofa when he came down the two steps leading to the living room, eating custard that she loathed; and she looked up to say, "I'll be as fat as a pig. All I've done for the last six days is eat gooey, slippery messes and drink gallons of milk. Sit down and I'll give you half of this."

"No, thanks. I'm planning on fried chicken later," he said to tease her, "and mashed potatoes and corn on the cob, topped off with apple pie à la mode."

"I get potatoes and ice cream," she returned equably, moving her feet so he could sit on the sofa with her. "And next week, if nothing hurts, I can add lots and lots of good things to my diet." And then she said, with what seemed a sudden change of thought, "You haven't seen our basement playroom since we brought the redwood furniture in from the porch and fixed it up for the winter. We'll go down later and have a rousing game of darts."

She had constantly wondered how she would entertain him. Tim wasn't the kind to sit still very long. He liked action, if it meant only driving about in his car. He didn't like to carpenter or fix leaky faucets, or fool around teaching Shadow new tricks. He was dear and he was fun, but she had never spent three whole days alone with him. She hadn't spent even one, because Spark Plug or some of the Cheltham gang had always been with them.

Spark Plug would be no trouble, she thought, tired and

listless from her long siege of pain. He would. . . . She resolutely thrust Spark Plug Blake from her mind. Tim was the one who had come rushing to her, bringing her roses and hovering over her as if she were a fragile figurine that might break. To push herself a little harder was the least she could do for him in return.

But Tim surprised her. He took one of the pillows from behind her head and laid a knitted afghan over her. "Now, you take a little nap, Ginger-cookie," he said. I've got a date with your mother in the kitchen. She's going to let me cut up stuff for the salad. We have some talking to do, so you won't mind if we close the door, will you?"

"Yes." Ginger was willing to rest because she knew she either had to do that or fall flat on her face, but she wanted to hear what was being said about her in the kitchen. "I'll be lonesome in here," she whined plaintively, knowing she sounded petulant and enjoying it. "You'll hash me over."

"I promise we won't, Scout's honor."

"Pooh. You weren't ever a boy scout, so that doesn't mean a thing. I think I'd better come out to the kitchen with you."

She sat up to lay the afghan aside but he gently shoved her down. "Ginger Johnston," he said sternly, "you're under doctor's orders. If you don't believe me, you can ask your father."

"Oh, go away." Ginger laughed, even though she resented such highhanded treatment. But she threatened, "I'll come out when I get good and ready. I'll only stay here until that darned old custard by-passes my ulcer."

Tim waited on her all that day and until sundown of the

next. Her parents would have, she knew, had they been given the chance, but Tim was always briskly ahead of them. He brought in her unappetizing tray, then spoonfed her when she gagged and rebelled, much like a father scooping food into a baby's mouth. He brought her up to date on the physics and history she had missed. He was so wonderfully sweet and such fun that when the telephone rang on Monday afternoon they went in to the library together, laughing, and without the slightest interest in who might be calling.

"Mrs. Johnston?" Spark Plug said on the other end of the line, not expecting to hear Ginger's voice. "How's Ginger?"

"Why, I'm fine," Ginger answered, suddenly conscious that Tim was the one who had picked up the receiver, spoken to the operator, and was listening. "Is anything wrong with you?"

"I'm worried to death."

Ginger had often thought that Spark Plug didn't need a telephone for his long-distance calls. His shouted words could carry anywhere within a thousand miles, so she clamped the receiver against her ear to dull them, and said needlessly to Tim, "It's Spark Plug."

"I got a special-delivery letter from Patty today," he went on, "and she wrote that you're practically at death's door. What's she raving about?"

"Well. . . ." Ginger hesitated briefly. Why tell him she had an ulcer, since Patty must already have done that? But perhaps Patty hadn't mentioned the name of the ailment. She rarely got anything straight. "Well," Ginger began again, "I had an ulcer." And she said to him, as she had to

Tim, "It was just a little ulcer and I think it's gone away now."

"Ulcers don't go away," he informed her. "They heal."

"So it's healed, then."

"And were you in the hospital, like Patty says?"

"Yep, I was. It was very nice there," she said conversationally. "Everything but the goop I had to eat."

"So how come you wrote to Patty and didn't tell me?" His voice was growing indignantly louder, and to reduce it to its normal shouting, she said:

"I didn't write to Patty. She called up and Mom told her where I was. If you'd called up," she said sweetly, "you'd have known, too."

"Umhum." He was chagrined but defensive, and he growled, "I'd have looked cute calling you up when you were all excited about your big football date with Tim. I'm not *that* stupid." There was sudden silence. Thick silence, like fog. Then he asked, "Who answered the telephone?"

"Oh, Tim did," Ginger returned, realizing in a flash what had been so wrong in the hospital, so different from any of the other times when she had been sick. No Spark Plug had been around to pop in and sit stiffly beside her bed, unafraid of catching her sniffles, her measles, or whatever she had. No pint of ice cream spooned sloppily into a cereal bowl, no daily delivery of her school assignments, no wilted flowers picked from her own garden, no scolding, no teasing, no urging her to get well so she could help him shovel snow or mow the grass. "He came Friday evening," she went on, rolling her eyes up at Tim who was patiently listening, even though he had picked up a book and was flicking its pages. "I couldn't persuade him to go on to the game, so he entertained me Saturday and brought me home yesterday morning. He's been awfully sweet to me."

They exchanged winks while Spark Plug asked in a coldly ferocious tone, "Is he planning to live there?"

"No, he has to leave right after dinner, worse luck." She saw Tim pointing toward the telephone, so nodded and said, "He wants to talk to you. Okay?"

"Put him on, but be sure you come back, because I don't want to spend my money yakking with him."

"Hi." Tim sat down on the arm of Ginger's chair, and she knew Spark Plug would yell bloody murder if he could see how close together they were.

"Our girl is coming along just fine," Tim said, sounding like the doctor on the case. "There's nothing to worry about now. She's out of the woods and on the mend. How are things with you?"

"Oh, so-so. You okay?"

"Yep."

"Then let me talk to Ginger again."

It had been a brief conversation, but Tim had known it would be, so he handed her the receiver and forgot to move. His arm lay across the back of her chair, her curls rested against his sleeve, and somewhere on the far end of a long string of telephone wire, Spark Plug was being frantically miserable.

CHAPTER NINE

MRS. JOHNSTON walked back along the driveway with Shadow bounding ahead of her. They had been to the post-box for the mail; and as she stood on the front steps in the pale, nippy November sunshine, she looked across the distant hills, wishing she hadn't let Ginger talk her into letting her go back to school. Ginger had also insisted on taking the bus as usual, doing everything just the way she always had, as if she hadn't been out for over a week.

"I do hope she'll be all right," she said to Shadow, who sat down on the step and grinned amiably. "Come on, it's time to make ourselves some lunch."

She had opened the door and was shooing Shadow in ahead of her when a car turned in at the gate and came up the driveway. It was an unfamiliar car, and she watched its progress. Then she saw two people in the front seat, and one of them was Ginger. The other was Mrs. Pierce.

"What happened?" she asked anxiously, running down the steps and meeting them as they got out and came toward her.

"Nothing to worry about," Mrs. Pierce answered. "Ginger had a little tummy upset, that's all."

"Oh, heavens!" Mrs. Johnston couldn't hold the exclamation back. How little Mrs. Pierce knew about ulcers if she could call what had happened to Ginger "a little tummy upset."

"It's all right, Mom, really it is," Ginger said, looking pale but cheerful. "I drank a Coke, that's all, and it made me sick for a few minutes." She was carrying her little basket that held the special foods she was to eat at noon, and she explained, "We were on our way to lunch, and, well—I forgot and drank the Coke. I'll eat this goop and I'll be all right."

"Hurry, then, and be sure to take your medicine." Mrs. Johnston watched Ginger bolt through the door. She wanted to follow, to get the medicine and unpack the basket as quickly as possible, but she had to stay and thank Mrs. Pierce. "It was so kind of you to bring her home," she said. "It isn't like Ginger to do something so foolish." And she suddenly shivered, from apprehension more than from the cold.

"May we go inside where I can talk to you for a few minutes?" Mrs. Pierce asked, seeing the involuntary shudder. And when they were standing in the hall with Mrs. Johnston taking her coat, she looked about and exclaimed, "What a lovely, lovely house you have!"

"Thank you," Mrs. Johnston said, wishing they could trade it for the smaller one in Cheltham, and straining to hear if Ginger was all right in the kitchen. "Shall we sit in the library? It's cozy on a day like this."

"And more private," Mrs. Pierce added, choosing one of the comfortable chairs and saying without preamble, "I want to explain this unfortunate occurrence to you and tell you why Ginger drank the Coca-Cola. I'm sure I know."

"Then please tell me, because I can't understand why, after all the child had been through, she would do such a thing. It baffles me."

"I think she drank it because Valerie offered it to her."

"*Valerie?*"

"Yes, it was the lunch hour. Our students aren't hurried, you know, so quite often they stop at one of our vending machines. The seniors had been very nice to Ginger all morning—that is, they asked her how she felt and she publicly thanked them for the flowers. I learned all this from Dr. Liebermann while I was waiting for Ginger to get her coat. Then, as she was walking to the dining room, Valerie separated herself from the group around the soft-drink machine and called, 'Hey, Ginger, come join us.' Betsy told me that. Mrs. Johnston," Mary Pierce leaned forward and asked, "what would you do if you were a seventeen-year-old girl who had been rejected by your schoolmates, then was suddenly asked to be one of them?"

"I suppose I'd have stopped," Mrs. Johnston said reluctantly, "but I would have been more careful than Ginger was. I wouldn't have drunk the Coke."

"No, I wouldn't, either, now that I'm old enough to know the consequences, but at Ginger's age I might have. I don't think Valerie did it maliciously," Mrs. Pierce said. "I can't bring myself to believe it for the simple reason that she could hardly have known what a carbonated drink might do to a person with an ulcer. I think she was trying to be friendly."

"I hope so. If you're right, this little setback probably won't do Ginger any permanent harm and it may heal a breach." Katherine Johnston wasn't entirely sure of Valerie's good intentions but she accepted them, and said, "Perhaps its best forgotten. Did any of the seniors seem upset?"

"They didn't know about it until I spoke to two or three. Valerie had gone on by then, and it was only luck that I happened in to check the girls' rest room for strays who might be smoking, and found Ginger there. Of course," she said, "I'll question them more thoroughly this afternoon."

Mrs. Johnston sat biting her lower lip as if clamping her teeth on a situation before she said, "Please don't. Let it drop. Ginger has a condition to contend with, and it's her responsibility to know what she can or can't do. I know she was eager to be included in the crowd around the machine so she did a foolish thing. She did it, Mrs. Pierce. Nobody forced her to, and she'll be back in school in a few days."

"I'll be back today." Ginger stood in the doorway, looking her perky self again. "I feel fine, Mom," she said. "Truly I do, and I want to go back."

"But let's give Mrs. Pierce some lunch first," her mother suggested, to postpone making a decision, "and then we can discuss it. She missed her own lunch by bringing you home."

"Oh, the teacher's dining room will still be open," Mrs. Pierce said, going out to the hall and taking her coat from a chair, "but I want Ginger to do what is best for her. Another day or two of rest won't hurt her, I'm sure."

"But I have to go back." Ginger's eyes pleaded with her mother and she begged, "Please, Mom. I can't let a little slip like this spoil—spoil everything."

Mrs. Johnston gave in. She didn't know what else to do with Mrs. Pierce present, but she did compromise by saying, "All right, but I'll come for you and we'll stop by Dr. Randolph's on our way home. I'll feel safer if we do that."

She stood in the door watching them drive away, then closed the door and leaned against it. "Why do I keep *temporizing?*" she asked herself desperately. "I let Ginger have Tim here all week end when I knew she should be quiet and rest; I let her go back to school when I felt sure she needs another week at home; and now this. Why, oh, why am I so weak? Is it just because I love her so much?"

Shadow padded in to sit in front of her. His smiling upturned face and wagging tail told her that she was a very wonderful person and that he approved of everything she did. He was so devoted all afternoon that she let him lie in the back of the station wagon when she started off for Paxton Hill.

Students were coming out when she stopped the car near the door. There were girls and boys of all ages, and many of them ran for the cars that were parked before and behind her. But there was no Ginger among them. Finally, when all the cars but hers had left, when the stream of students was reduced to a trickle, to couples, to sometimes one alone, she still waited in an agony of apprehension. And when she could bear it no longer, she said, "Stay, Shad," and ran along the walk toward the school.

Ginger was just coming into the big hall. Her coat was open, she carried her books clasped against her, and her eyes were shining like stars. "Oh, gosh, Mom," she cried, "I'm sorry you had to wait!"

"It's all right, darling. You weren't sick again, were you?"

"Mercy, no." Ginger let her mother take her books even though they weren't heavy, and said, "I was busy being appointed to things."

"Appointed to things? What kind of things?" Mrs. Johnston asked, puzzled.

"Well, they weren't much, but they're a beginning. Mr. Landers—he's the head of the English department and our faculty adviser—asked me if I'd be on the newspaper staff. Burke had already asked me and I wouldn't, but Mr. Landers is different. He's a teacher. So I said I'd try, and he told me I'd have to read over the stuff that comes in, decide what's good, and edit it. He's been doing it but he really hasn't the time. I had to wait while he explained everything to me and gave me that Manila envelope you're carrying. Oh, Mom, we'll have staff meetings twice a week," she said proudly. Then her eyes clouded like the sky on a dull winter day, and she said, "Mr. Landers was the one who asked me, and he'll be at all the meetings, so nobody can think I'm pushy, can they?"

"No, honey," her mother answered, " but it seems like such a lot for you to take on, just now."

"It isn't. It's good for me." Ginger saw Shadow in his glass cage and flung open the door to let him hang over the second seat and lick her face. "Hi, old boy," she said, laying her cheek against his brown ruff. Then she closed the door again and sat in her own place beside her mother.

"Something else happened," she said, "but it wasn't what delayed me. Valerie asked me to be on the committee for our first dance and do the decorations."

"Honey, she knows you can't."

"Well, she asked. That's something, isn't it? She stopped

me in the hall and said, 'I'm sorry about offering you that Coke,' and I said, 'My goodness, it isn't your fault if I'm stupid.' And then she asked me."

Ginger leaned back against the seat and closed her eyes as if suddenly weary. "Mom," she said, "I've made progress. I hate to think it all happened because I got sick, but I suppose I'll have to admit that it did. Daddy's paid my tuition, and because the school doesn't want to refund it, the teachers got busy. It's sort of pitiful, isn't it?"

"Yes," her mother answered, not knowing what else to say.

"But I'll prove myself. I'll be an honor student, and I'll do good work on the newspaper and the yearbook—so what do I have to cry about?"

Shadow jumped over onto the seat behind her and licked her neck to show how much he loved her; and turning to give him a pat, she said, "Thanks, pal, for your vote of confidence."

CHAPTER TEN

GINGER'S school days were moving along satisfactorily, but her social life remained at a standstill. She thoroughly enjoyed the editorial sessions because they were informal yet busy, and Mr. Landers was always there. Her rejection by her class had made her so self-conscious and shy that she thought of Mr. Landers as a chaperon, and addressed most of her remarks to him. He, in turn, delegated the greater part of the work to her. She was given a weekly column. It was a news column, discussing world happenings in a light way that the newspaper's younger readers could understand, and was headed *Ginger's Seeing Eye*. Burke had thought up the title, and while she would have preferred *Let's Look at the News*, with her name left off, she accepted it and thanked him.

Valerie had thought the publishing business hopelessly dull and had dropped out, so Ginger became assistant editor without portfolio or title. Valerie's defection had taken place before someone had had the bright idea of sending out for sandwiches and cold drinks so she didn't know what fun she was missing, and Ginger drank milk and scooped the filling from a piece of custard pie to the pleasant jeering of her co-workers. She loved every minute of it, and on the days of the conferences, drove the station wagon to school.

"I don't want them to think I'm hanging around for a ride home," she said to her mother when she finally accepted the offer of the car. "I'm thrilled to death with what I'm doing, but it's better to be independent and not take any chances on being popped back in the doghouse again. I've begun to like Burke, I really have, because he's a lot smarter than he pretends to be. But I'm keeping our relations on a business basis."

So she studied and worked on her column at night, did her editing, and plodded on in what her parents considered a dreary way. She even gained three pounds.

Spark Plug telephoned every week, Tim now and then, and Patty whenever her allowance could be stretched to a call. And then, quite suddenly, it was the week of Thanksgiving.

"Ginger," Patty shrilled excitedly into the telephone on Monday evening, "can you come up here? Spark Plug and Tim will be home, and Jane and Fred and Bill and Betsy Barns and Chipper Tartler, and of course Steve and Mary Lou will be around, so I'm going to have a party. You'll have to answer quickly because I can't afford but three minutes. Can you come?"

"Why, I don't know," Ginger gasped, thrilled with the excitement of such an unexpected adventure. I'll have to talk to Mom and Daddy about it." And then she asked, "How would I get there?"

"On the train, silly," Patty shot back. "Please say you'll come. I can't have the party if you don't."

"I'll call you back. I'll call you back in half an hour," Ginger promised.

She replaced the receiver with Patty still talking and raced into the living room. "I know you heard," she said in breathless haste. "Patty wants me to come up for the Thanksgiving week end. May I go?"

"Oh, honey," her mother started to answer, then let her gaze rest on her husband as she always did in a crisis. "Why don't you ask them to come here?" she suggested, hoping he would back her up.

"Because they've already been here and we haven't anything more to do that's fun. Oh, Mom—Daddy. . . ." Ginger threw herself on her knees at her father's feet and rested her cheek against his knee. "I just *have* to go!" she cried desperately. "I have to go *back*. Haven't you ever felt," she asked, looking up, "that you must go back to a place where you were happy, just to see what it's still like? To see if it's as wonderful as you remember it, or if you can put it out of your mind?"

"Yes," he answered, stroking her hair, "and a month ago we would have sent you off and been happy about it. We even thought of asking the Palmers to keep you and let you go to school there. Now, with this ulcer business. . . ."

"But it's almost gone," Ginger said, looking straight at him. "I'm sticking to my diet and Dr. Randolph says I'm fine. Oh, Daddy, can't we call Dr. Randolph and ask him? Let him decide."

She knew in her heart what the understanding doctor's answer would be, so pressed her point, crawling back and forth from one parent to the other, hugging Shadow on her way and promising to eat nothing but the foods Dr. Randolph prescribed. And within the promised half-hour, she had Patty on the telephone again to tell her she could come.

"I'll take the two o'clock train from here," she said,

trying to keep the excited quiver out of her voice. "It gets in at four-seventeen, and I'll be the girl with the broad grin who leaps off into space."

"Oh, swell! Gosh, that's *swell!*" Patty cried in answer. And she remembered to add, "Bring lots of clothes, because it's going to be gay."

Ginger knew what clothes she would need in Cheltham, because, as she reminded Patty, she had lived there for almost seventeen years. So she packed sweaters and skirts, her blue school blazer, should she want to show off to the Blakes some morning, two wool dresses, and almost as an afterthought, the swishy peach evening frock she had worn to the deadly dull dance Tim had taken her to last summer.

"Well, that's it," she said, watching her father carry two cases out to the car. "I'll be back on Sunday evening at six-thirty. I'm so excited I'm about to pop."

Never had a train seemed so slow. It was an express that made only two stops as it hustled toward Philadelphia, but to Ginger it loitered unnecessarily in the stations. Would Spark Plug arrive ahead of her? she wondered, watching scenery fly past. Would Tim? Spark Plug had said he would drive east with a friend who was going to New York for the holidays, and Tim should be there by now. Would they be surprised to see her or would Patty have given the whole thing away by writing more of her special-delivery letters? Would the college crowd have changed? Would Mary Lou come racing over? How would the back of her own dear house look from Patty's bedroom window? And the Blakes', next door to it?

She became so busy asking herself questions and telling herself over and over in wonderment, "I'm going back, I'm actually going back," that the train slid into the long dark tunnel leading to the Thirtieth Street station before she had her coat on.

Patty, Mary Lou, and Steve were on the platform: Mary Lou still round as a dumpling, Patty forgetting to be beautiful in her excitement, and blond, snub-nosed Steve. They were peering in all the windows that passed, and when she leaned toward the glass and waved, they marched along beside the slowly moving train, making a frightful racket. Mary Lou had a comb wrapped in tissue paper, Steve beat on a toy drum, Patty clapped two tin lids together, and they all sang a badly rehearsed "Happy Days Are Here Again." Ginger, flinging herself at them, added her shriek of excitement to their din.

"Oh, it's wonderful!" and "I can't believe it!" they all cried over and over, while she hugged them, Steve, too, in her excitement. They partially blocked the path of a few amused passengers who were boarding the train, and Patty added, "Oh, Ginger, you've actually come home!"

Patty was about to cry, in the easy, beautiful way she had learned to do it: her blue eyes wide open, her mouth holding a controlled smile instead of stretched into a childish O. And to stop the tears that were so easily turned on but took a lot of doing to turn off, Ginger said quickly, "Oh, golly, I forgot my suitcases."

"I have them." Steve took them from the porter and teased, "I see you travel first class, madam."

"Oh, it was Mom's and Daddy's idea," Ginger retorted, wrinkling her nose at him. Then, because she thought it better to let them know quickly that she was still in the semi-invalid class, she said, "They thought I might faint or need a glass of milk or something. I'm back to normal, really."

"You look kind of skinny to me," Mary Lou said enviously, as they went up to the station on the escalator. "I lost a pound and a half last month but I gained a pound back this week."

"I never gain or lose," Patty remarked with unctuous satisfaction, moving up to the same step with Ginger, which was a hostess's right. "We came in Mother's new station wagon because Steve's old rattletrap car is too dangerous, Mother thought."

"You could have come in a truck for all I care," Ginger answered, when they were all together again and walking across a marble floor to the vast area of parking spaces. "Tell me about the party. Will everybody be there?"

"Of course. You don't think I'd do anything *halfway*, do you?" Patty was herself again, and standing under the porte-cochere while Steve went off for the car, she said, "Mother engaged a couple to run the house for the whole week end, so we'll dress tonight—in formals, I mean—and Craig Vandergriff's combo band is coming at nine o'clock to play for dancing down in the playroom. And we can hold open house whenever we want to."

"Oh." The first twinge of misgiving struck Ginger. This wouldn't be Cheltham; this dressing up and formal entertaining wouldn't resemble the life she had lived. What had happened to Patty? She had sounded so normal and like herself on the telephone, even when she met the train and clapped her tin lids together, and now she was behaving like a Washington debutante. The Palmers could no more afford such richness than could the Johnstons. It was all disturbing, and not even a broad wink from Mary Lou quite restored her enthusiasm.

Patty's parents did, a little. They were so unaffectedly glad to see her, and Mrs. Palmer stood with her arm about Ginger's shoulders, waiting while Ginger looked across the back lawns and wintry hedges at the white clapboard house that had once been hers.

"It hasn't changed, dear," she said, "but sometimes I think it has a waiting look, as if it's hoping the Johnstons will come back and live in it. Houses have a way of belonging to people."

"Yes," Ginger answered, grateful for the understanding. There was her old, dear driveway with Spark Plug's house next to it, and there was Heidi sitting on the back steps. "Oh, Mrs. Palmer," she blurted out, "I do miss living here so much. I know it's wrong, but I want everything to be the way it used to be."

She couldn't cry as beautifully as Patty, so she brushed away two big rolling tears and tried to sound happy as she answered Patty's peremptory call from the front door. She even exclaimed properly over Patty's new suite that had been made by adding her older brother Douglas's room to hers.

"Do you think it's as pretty as yours?" Patty asked anxiously, while Ginger stood looking at the new furniture, new draperies, new everything.

"Yes, it's much nicer than mine," Ginger answered dutifully, wishing she could see some single piece of furniture left from the past, or that she could have a few free minutes to go wandering through a house that was an exact duplicate of the one she had grown up in. But she must unpack in a hurry, Patty said, and the new maid must press Ginger's dress because Mary Lou and Steve would be back in a little while, and all the others with them.

Why, oh, why is she doing it this way? Ginger wondered, letting the soft peach-colored folds of the dress drift down around her. Why can't we go tearing around the way we used to? Why can't I run over to the Blakes to say hello and see if Spark Plug's come yet? Why do we have to be so *stylish?*

The blue draperies had been drawn across the windows and she and Patty were enclosed in an unfamiliar room, putting on unfamiliar clothes, turning themselves into unfamiliar people. Patty danced about in her new blue dress, and Ginger audibly admired her. Once I'd have said, "Oh, don't be so vain," Ginger told the bathroom mirror. "Now I can't. We're as polite to each other as if we'd never made mud pies together."

But when the other guests began to arrive it was better. Patty played the part of perfect hostess, and Ginger was free to greet each one with shrieks of joy. Jeff Alexander had grown some long, lush sideburns for a college western he was to be in; Jane McGuire and Fred Eikoff were still engaged and would be married after Christmas, then finish college together. The high school crowd wanted to know about her school, what she did, and how she liked the social life in Washington. And when she laughingly confessed that she did nothing and had no social life, they wouldn't believe her.

It was almost seven-thirty when Tim rang the doorbell. "Sorry to be late," he said to Patty in the hall. "Spark Plug's ride let him off ten miles from home and I had to go out and pick him up." Then he saw Ginger in the living room and said, "Hi, all," and made straight for her.

"If it isn't my little Ginger-cookie!" he shouted joyfully, taking the hands she held out to him, "Why, gosh, you look fine, Ginger-cookie."

"I feel wonderful," she answered; and before she knew it he had put his arm around her waist and turned her toward the others.

"None of you may know it, but this was one sick kid," he said, taking her with him as he toured the long room, speaking to those he hadn't yet seen. And he told Mary Lou and Steve, "When I saw her lying in that hospital bed I said to myself, 'Tim, my friend, you're going to stay right here this week end and do a job of mending.' "

Ginger laughed, even while she vehemently denied that she had been as sick as Tim was making out. She did wish he would release her before Spark Plug came, but since he always hugged all the girls in public, and put his arm around Mary Lou's thick waist as often as anyone else's, she knew it was just his Timmish way of being friendly. Then the swinging door between the dining room and kitchen banged open and whooshed shut. She recognized that bang and whoosh.

Spark Plug had come charging through the kitchen because he was in a hurry. Ginger was the one he wanted to see and the first one he singled out—and she was standing with her back to him, plastered against Tim like a wilted paper doll. How could he know that her heart was beating like a snare drum, that she felt his presence and was trying to break loose and turn around? All he saw was that she and Tim turned together as a team.

"Hi, Spark Plug," everyone said, converging on him. He was surrounded, and in sudden anger at Ginger, he made the most of it. He even gave Patty extra attention and, unheard of for him, admired her blue dress. Ginger's peach-and-whipped-cream confection went unnoticed, as did her recent illness, when he said, "Hello, there, Ginger. You're looking good. I thought you'd been sick."

"Not recently." Ginger gave him a tremulous little smile that he should have been able to read and wished he would at least shake hands with her. She wanted her hand to rest comfortably in his, cozy and safe, the way she had planned for it to. But it didn't.

Everyone went into the dining room that had been cleared to make space for five white-decked card tables; and sitting with Tim, Jane, and Fred, she felt as if Spark Plug were a million light miles away. His back was almost touching hers, and while each could hear everything the other said, they were on separate planets. She was on Earth, somewhere down in a deep pit and gasping for air, and he was happily zooming about in orbit.

It was a fine homecoming, she thought miserably, while she undressed for bed. She had danced with every boy but Spark Plug, her head aching from the twang of a guitar, a set of racketing drums and the Palmers' out-of-tune piano. Tim had guarded her health while Spark Plug, whose job had always been to look after her, neither noticed how tired she was nor that she always happened to end a dance near him.

The evening had been a total waste. It wasn't Patty's fault, she thought loyally, slapping her dress back in her suitcase where it would stay until she went home. Patty had gone all out for an elegant, sophisticated evening. And it had cost a lot. It had been Patty's idea of the smart way to entertain, and she was dizzily happy with the result.

"Yes, the boys certainly did give you a rush," Ginger answered tiredly, when Patty sat on the side of her bed, putting her hair up on rollers to be ready for whatever tomorrow might bring. "You really had what it takes."

"I thought so," Patty agreed complacently and stretched her arms above her head. "Mary Lou's silly steak fry is going to be awfully sloppy after this," she said, "but it's about the way Mary Lou would do things. Good gracious!" she exclaimed. "Why do you keep looking out the back window?"

"I don't know." Ginger wished she were braver. Her old house was back there, the house she had come to see, so why couldn't she say so? A light was on in the Blake kitchen, so why couldn't she say casually, "I can see Spark Plug moving around and fixing himself a late snack. Do you mind if I run over for a minute?" She couldn't; not to this strange new Patty, so she drew the curtains again and sat down to take off her slippers.

Tomorrow might be better, she thought wistfully. Perhaps she could get up while Patty was still asleep and run over to the Blakes'. Just as she always had—charging in and demanding, "You big lug, what made you act like such a square last night?" She would be good and mad, and wouldn't care how many members of the Blake family were around to hear her, because they'd heard her before. She could get to the bottom of Spark Plug's unspeakable behavior if she had on a sweater and skirt and could look and act like herself. Or could she? She hadn't done so well with her classmates this year, her miserable thoughts reminded her, so how could she hope to crash in on Spark Plug and tell him what was what?

"I can't," she whispered to herself, hunched under a new pink blanket; and then she added dutifully, "But I'll have to. I'll just—have to." And she pulled herself up against her pillow to say for the dozenth time, "Yes, Patty, it was the loveliest party I ever went to, truly it was. Everybody had the most marvelous time and I don't see how you ever did it."

CHAPTER ELEVEN

PATTY actually did sleep late the next morning. When Ginger slipped out of bed and looked across at her, Patty was face down in her pillow, which, Ginger decided, was the only way she could sleep comfortably, owing to the rows and rows of hard, round rollers. Padded satin hangers slid noiselessly along a rod in the closet, unlike the Johnstons' jangle of wire hangers from the cleaner's, and Ginger was able to take out a gray skirt, a blouse and sweater, and then her camel's-hair coat without waking her roommate.

She could hear Mr. and Mrs. Palmer talking in their bedroom and sounds of activity in the kitchen, so she dressed quietly and slipped out the front door.

Even from the driveway, she could see her destination. She would step over the low hedge that bordered the Blakes' back yard instead of taking the one beyond it that was sparse from so many years of little girls squeezing through it. It would be a short journey but one that was filled with memories.

The dry, spongy grass felt the same to her slowly moving feet, but there was no Shadow to bark a joyous morning welcome at her early return. The trash cans behind the new owner's garage still had JOHNSTON painted on them, but they stood upright and were tightly sealed because a big brown dog had moved away. A strange car was parked in the familiar driveway and a strange atmosphere pervaded everything. Ginger felt as if she were a haunting ghost trying desperately to re-enter her past. Silence, dead silence. No loving, living human being remained. Then, like the lonesome little ghost she was, she opened the Blakes' back door, and Heidi began to yelp in hysterical, welcoming barks.

There was the homey smell of turkey roasting in the oven, the aroma of coffee bubbling in the percolator, the acrid odor of toast almost burned, which was the way the Blakes liked it, the fragrance of a kitchen that was lived in. Ginger knew she had come home at last, even before several pairs of loving arms reached out to receive her.

Spark Plug wasn't there. He and his father had driven over to the bowling alley to see how Styx was doing without his trusted helper, Mrs. Blake explained, while Dodie and Debbie hovered about, offering jam and bacon, and filling a cereal bowl so full that toasted grains of wheat spilled over on the breakfast cloth.

Ginger was eager for Spark Plug to come home, but dreaded it, too. The fight would start then, so it was pleasant to sit in the breakfast nook, listening to the chatter around her and telling about her school and her ulcer.

Then she heard a car door slam. One set of footsteps came around the house, the right set, and in her nervousness she dropped her piece of toast buttered side down for Heidi to snatch.

"Say, Mom, I left Dad. . . ." Spark Plug began before he saw Ginger. Then he closed the door and came over to stand beside the table. "What brought you out so early?" he asked.

"I came to have breakfast with your family and to find out what made you act so awful last night."

"I thought I was charming." Spark Plug took off his car coat, parked it on top of the refrigerator, and pulled out a chair to sit down. "I certainly did make with the charm," he said to his mother, who was silently signaling "o-u-t" to Debbie and Dodie. "You would have been proud of your boy, Mrs. Blake, so social he was."

"Oh, stop it." Ginger didn't care if the rest of the family left or not, but she said to their departing backs, "He was perfectly horrid. He didn't dance with me, not even once."

"I'll have to give him a lesson on being polite," Mrs. Blake said, turning to wink, "even when he's jealous."

"I didn't think she ought to dance so much," Spark Plug shouted, although the dining-room door had swung shut. "If she's been as sick as Tim constantly told everyone she was, I thought she should sit down once in a while and take it easy."

"I did," Ginger retorted, leaning her elbows on the table and staring at him. "And every time I sat near where you were, you moved your big old self somewhere else."

"I was making with my charm."

"Not to me." She put a piece of bread in the toaster, then went back to looking at him. "What happened to my big buddy that I came all this way to see?" she asked.

"Tim? Why he was right beside you, dancing with you,

guiding your faltering footsteps here and there," he answered. "Oh, boy, was he!"

Spark Plug had also hoped a showdown would come. He had hoped Ginger would tell him off because that was the only way he could know if she was still his Ginger. He had hurried to the party as fast as he could, with his socks mismatched and tying his tie as he went. And what had he found? Tim there before him. Tim, who had dressed early, who had only to park his car after his errand of mercy, and walk in.

"It was all Patty's fault," he said, knowing Ginger would follow his thoughts. "I looked good. I had on my new sports jacket to impress my folks, then Tim said you were here and Patty was giving a party for you. She had made a great point of its being a dressy affair, Tim said, and when Patty makes a point, she means it. So I had to hustle in and put on my dark suit. And that made me late. And what did I find when I finally got there?" he asked, suddenly belligerent again.

"You found me with my heart thumping like mad and trying to get loose to run meet you. *That's* what you found." A piece of bread popped up in the toaster, and she took it out, laid it on a plate and buttered it while she said, "And if you didn't have sense enough to know what you found you should have pretended you did. It was mean of you to ruin my first evening back in Cheltham. All I could think of all evening, and all night, too, was, Oh, I wish I hadn't come. I *wish* I hadn't come. Here." She shoved the plate at him and gave him the dish of jelly.

Spark Plug couldn't have eaten the toast had he been starving. "I did talk to you—some," he muttered.

"Yes, you did. Whenever people were around and you knew I couldn't ask you what I'd done to make you mad, you mumbled at me. But you didn't care one single bit how I felt."

"Ginger, listen while I try to explain." Spark Plug cleared the space before him and crossed his arms on the table so his face could come closer to hers. "I know this sounds corny," he said, "but I went through a bad time when you were sick and Tim was down there. Tim's a good guy, but he likes you too much, and he was there. I got to thinking. . . ."

"He wasn't there one bit more than if he'd taken me to the football game," she interrupted. "You knew I was planning to go to the game with him."

"Yes, but this was different," he went on. "I know how sweet and tender Tim can be. I've seen him in action. How did I know bùt what you. . . ."

A second interruption seemed in order, so she said, "That was over a month ago, and I've talked to you on the telephone at least six times since. I've told you that Tim was nice to me. I've even told you how tired I got from trying to be nice to him."

"Yeah, that's true. I believed you. I worried about you so much that I fluffed a writ, and I kept telling myself, 'She's going to be all right, she's going to be *all right.*' "

"Well, I am." Ginger smiled into his misery of self-revelation, but he went on:

"And when I walked in to that party, what were you doing?"

"I was hooked to Tim," she answered honestly. "To kind, bumbling, Dr. Mark Timberlake, III. He really believes he's taking over for Dr. Randolph this week end. Do you think I *liked* being followed around—lots more than Mom and Daddy would have done—and being told not to dance, not to move? If I'd had on shorts instead of that darned long dress I might have deliberately stood on my head."

"He was trying," Spark Plug said, unconsciously praising his rival instead of blaming him.

"So was I. So was everybody but you." Ginger's emotions had run the gamut. She had pitied herself, had pitied Spark Plug, and now she was angry again. "You're just plain *selfish!*" she cried. And she watched Mrs. Blake poke her head around the dining-room door.

"I'm sorry," Mrs. Blake apologized, "but I have to look at my turkey. Go right on with your fight and don't mind me."

"It's over." Ginger got up from her chair and pulled her coat around her. "You're such nice people," she said, "that I don't see how you ever got such a mean son." Then she marched to the door and out.

"Ginger!"

Spark Plug was running after her. She had known he would, so her exit hadn't been as dramatic as it had looked. "Yes?" she said icily, sounding as cold as the Thanksgiving morning.

"Do you want me to take you to Mary Lou's tonight?" he asked, catching up.

"If you'd like to." She walked on slowly. Her head ached and she wished she were home. Tears were on the verge of sprouting behind her eyes, and she said with a groan, "I don't see why I ever came back to this silly place, why I was so homesick for it. I've felt strange and miserable ever since I got here. I don't like it and I want to go home."

"Aw, honey child." Spark Plug stopped her as she reached the Palmers' back steps. "It's going to be better," he promised. "We'll have fun at Mary Lou's tonight, we always do; and I'll ask our special gang over tomorrow night for one of our old-time ping-pong sessions."

"Steve is having a party," she said dully. "The catering gang is transferring itself over there. I don't see why everybody has to be so *fancy* suddenly."

"It's because of you," he said, watching her go up the steps and then come down again to make a proper entrance through the front door. "If you don't believe me, ask Mary Lou."

"I will." She stood in the cold, shivering a little, and she said, "Yes, I suppose I'm to blame. It's a habit I seemed to have formed."

"Do you want to go bowling this afternoon?"

"I can't." Her eyes had never looked bigger or more wistful as she said, "We're having the big Thanksgiving dinner at two o'clock—in four courses, Patty told me—but I can be ready by five-thirty. That's when Mary Lou said to come. Steve's picking up Patty, so if you want to come for me you can. 'By, for now." She walked around the house without once looking back at him or at the trash cans marked JOHNSTON.

"Where have you been?" Patty cried when she opened the front door. "Helga kept your breakfast hot until I told her not to. After all," she reminded in a superior tone, "she has dinner to cook."

"That I know." Ginger, from years of moving about in a house that was a twin to this one, turned in to the long hall that led to the bedrooms. "Come on," she said, "let's make our beds."

"Oh, goodness, Helga did it." Patty followed, airily exclaiming as she walked along, "I have so many things I want to show you: new clothes, pictures of the Halloween dance, and loads of snapshots we've taken of the gang at picnics and parties."

Ginger felt cold again. Sitting with Patty in her fancy little sitting room, looking at evidence of the wonderful summer and fall Patty had had, she realized with a jolt that all their conversations through the years had been centered on Patty. Today was no different. Patty couldn't have understood Ginger's difficult year at school if she had wanted to, or sympathized with it, either. She would merely say at the end of a short recital, as she had so often on the telephone, "Well, my goodness, Ginger, you ought to go to more parties and have fun. It's silly to shut yourself up and study, and not make friends. I miss having you here but I don't let it *stop* me."

No, Spark Plug and her parents had been right all these years. She was nothing but a sounding board to Patty. The discovery made her feel empty and sad.

The Thanksgiving dinner went off in fine style. Mr. Palmer read a cablegram from Douglas in Paris, the florist delivered a large pot of golden chrysanthemums, sent by Ginger's parents, the turkey was superb, the plum pudding came in flaming, and Ginger was encouraged to tell about her life in Vienna. She talked more at dinner than she had in all the twenty-four hours she had been in Cheltham, freely, and, surprising to her, with a nostalgic homesickness for a place she had been eager to leave.

Spark Plug arrived on time, looking more like himself in his new tweed jacket and slacks, and Ginger flung on her coat and ran out to the car with him. She had put on one of her school skirts and a white, round-collared blouse. Then, instead of slipping on the blue mohair cardigan she had laid out, she had chosen her school blazer.

"It's a status symbol," she had laughingly said to Patty, who favored Ginger's new beige wool. And to Patty's blank incomprehension she added, "So I'll know who I am." Patty, in rustling plaid silk, was patiently waiting for Steve to come for her.

Mary Lou's parties were always informal. Her big, rambling three-storied house was usually filled with little brothers and their dogs, big brothers with their wives and children, so Mary Lou's guests always clattered straight to the basement. There were three rooms down there. One smallish one was equipped for table tennis; another, a little larger, was a combination laundry room and makeshift kitchen; and the big room, with its odds and ends of furniture, had a fireplace that ran the entire length of one wall. There was a grill at the end of the fireplace, and Mary Lou, in a chef's cap and apron, was an expert at grilling hamburgers.

Tim was wearing the chef's cap by the time Ginger and Spark Plug arrived, and was piling more charcoal on the fire. "Hi," he looked around to say without stopping his work. "Put in your order. Do you like your hamburger well done or raw?"

"Medium," Ginger answered, nipping off the cap and setting it back on his head at a rakish angle.

She had talked with Tim at noon and they understood

each other completely. "Old Spark was pretty burned last night," he had said on the telephone. "It didn't bother you, did it?"

"Yes," Ginger had answered frankly. And she had added, "I think you were showing off just to irritate him. We're straightened out now, so please behave yourself."

"I will," he had promised. "I truly will, Ginger-cookie. I love old Spark and I wouldn't make him come unglued for the world, and you know it."

"Then be a good boy," she said. "He's coming to pick me up, so go on to the party and act like your nice, kind self."

She supposed Tim thought they were conspiring together, but it didn't matter. Spark Plug was happy, and she was the happiest she had been since she came back to Cheltham. Mary Lou's party was so like old times, with one group throwing darts, another batting a little celluloid ball back and forth on a rickety table, and the old record player scratching away.

The same twenty guests were there, but the basement wasn't crowded. Everybody carried his or her used paper plate and cup to the big corrugated trash can in the laundry-kitchen and dropped stainless steel forks and spoons into a laundry tub. Ginger, wandering out after dinner, found Mary Lou picking up scattered paper napkins that had fallen out of the holder.

"Mary Lou," she said, stooping to retrieve a napkin from under an old-fashioned washing machine, "tonight has been what I came back to find. It's—it's Cheltham."

"What's gone before hasn't been, huh?" Mary Lou pushed her untidy hair out of her eyes and took the napkin. "I was kind of afraid you'd be in for a shock," she answered.

"I loved the first part—that silly band you thought up when you met me and the feeling that I'd come home again. Then, when we got to Patty's, I—something was all changed, Mary Lou. I don't mean just the dressing up," she explained, "because we've always loved to go swishing around in formals, but such a fuss was made about everything. I felt like a guest at the White House."

"You know why, don't you?" Mary Lou asked frankly. And when Ginger shook her head in a puzzled way, she went on, "Patty's envious, Ginger. She envies you your new house and your private school." And at Ginger's look of dismay, she said, "Yes, she does. She thinks you have a lot of expensive things that she doesn't, so she tried to make all of us who went to your house party spruce up and entertain you in a bang-up way. I wouldn't, and Tim can't because his grandmother isn't up to it, and Spark Plug wasn't here, but she made Steve come through in style, and she sure did."

"Oh, no!" Ginger pulled a folding chair out from the oilcloth-covered table and sat down on it. "Do you mean," she asked, "that Patty made her mother hire *servants* just to wait on me while I'm here?"

"Yep."

"I feel awful."

"Don't." Mary Lou shook her head and advised, "Don't let it worry you. Mr. Palmer is making heaps of money. He has to be if he can send Douglas to Paris to take his junior year of college, and can rent a cottage at the shore again next summer. Patty wants him to buy the Severson house;

it's the biggest one around here, and Daddy thinks he has it sold to him. Cheltham Manor isn't good enough for Patricia now, not since she's seen where you live."

"If she only knew!"

"And she can't talk of any school but Smith or Vassar. I," Mary Lou said grinning, "will be grateful to go to Drexel and commute from home."

"I can't believe it." Ginger sat straight on her wobbly chair, and cried, "Not Patty! Why, we've grown up together. We each got a new coat every other spring and fall; we carried out the garbage, and I still do. We were happy and proud to live where we did. Surely, just because I happened to move to a larger house, she wouldn't be so stupid. You have to be wrong, Mary Lou."

"I'm not." Mary Lou knew the truth and was determined to make Ginger believe it. "I wouldn't have told you," she said, "if you hadn't been disappointed with your visit." And she changed the subject by asking, "Can you come over and spend tomorrow night with me?"

"I can't possibly," Ginger said with a sigh. "But I won't be so uncomfortable now that I know what the trouble is. I'll accept the fine service and make a great show of enjoying the luxury. You know," she said as they went back to join the others, "Spark Plug told me that all the fancy fuss was for me, but I misunderstood him. I thought he meant that I had changed some way and was personally to blame. It gave my inferiority complex an awful plunge."

"Well, don't let it. You're high society around here—to Patty, at least, and there'll be quite a blurb in the local newspaper. 'Miss Virginia Johnston of Washington, D.C., and Virginia,' " she pretended to quote, " 'is the house guest of Miss Patricia Palmer. Miss Palmer entertained lavishly with a dinner party and dancing. Music was furnished by the Combo Four, and the young ladies were dressed in formal attire. Miss Palmer wore a blue gown of soup-de-blooey, et cetera, et cetera.' Just the way Mattie Billingsly writes everything."

Ginger burst out laughing at dear, comic Mary Lou. She felt as she had a year ago; and when Tim appeared beside her and whispered, "Do you think Spark Plug will fall apart if we dance together?" she whispered back, "Let's go over and ask him."

Spark Plug and Steve were putting a four-foot log on the dying fire in the fireplace, and she leaned over to ask in a sweet, coaxing simper, "Mr. Blake, sir, will you fall apart if I dance with Mr. Ford?"

"Nope," he turned to say over his shoulder; then he straightened up and grinned. "But just one dance," he stipulated. "And I reserve the right to cut in."

"Why, Mr. Blake." Ginger clapped her hand over her mouth in feigned amazement. "Fancy *you* dancing," she said, "and with little old me." Then, as she went off with Tim, she called back, "Thanks, old buddy."

CHAPTER TWELVE

GINGER was glad she had gone back to Cheltham, even though part of a beautiful dream was dead. Patty never could quite be Patty again, the winsome, selfish, naughty Patty she had thought she knew. That Patty was gone, and Ginger wondered if she could ever feel close to the new, arrogant one.

So much was gone, she told herself, plodding back and forth to school, and it was foolish to have tried to hold on to it. To clutch it, really, taking out memories and putting them back, hoarding them like a miser with a cache of old dollar bills. New money was being minted, new experiences were coming her way, and it was her duty to be grateful for them and receptive.

So, inch by slow inch she gained stature in her class. Not socially, she admitted with amusement, because although George had invited her to the pre-Christmas dance, he developed measles and they couldn't go; but as a student and part of a working organization.

Burke telephoned her now and then in the evening for advice on the newspaper, and twice he came over to work with her on a special feature they were doing together for the yearbook. She kept the visits businesslike and as short as possible, and didn't offer him hot chocolate or a cola. She knew he wanted to stay on after their work was finished, but she never suggested it. And the night his car got stuck in a snowdrift on the curving driveway, she stood at a window and watched him work his way out instead of going out to shovel with him as she would have liked to do.

And then Christmas came. It brought a new collar for Shadow and an almost-new car for her. The car was one of the larger compacts, and good old Santa Claus had left it in the driveway, wrapped in clear plastic and tied with wide red ribbon.

"My goodness, I won't have to ride that darned bus any more!" she cried, jumping up and down with excitement. And the first thought she had was, Oh, how will I ever tell Patty? Then she heard the telephone ringing inside and went skidding off to answer it.

"Merry Christmas," Spark Plug said. "Did you like my present?"

"You didn't send me any." Ginger had torn the heavy wrapping paper from the Blakes' big package, looking for a box, any sized box that had a card from Spark Plug on it. No perfume, no stationery, no scarf or handkerchiefs this year. "What happened?" she asked. "Did your mother forget to buy you something to send me?"

"I'm bringing it."

"You're *what?*"

He had expected stunned silence, not the shriek that almost broke his eardrum, and he hurried to say, "Tim and I thought we'd drive down for a couple of days if you want us."

The Siamese twins. Neither could let the other out of his sight, and Ginger's laughter bubbled over the wire. "When?" she asked breathlessly.

"Well. . . ." Spark Plug had broken his news and now it would be fun to keep her in suspense. "We've taken part in all the doings at home," he finally said, "so we thought. . . ."

More silence. Indistinct voices and laughter, then Tim broke in to say: "We're on our way, Ginger-cookie. The idea hit us all of a sudden, so we'll pack our gear and be on our way in half an hour. If you really want us, that is."

"Want you? Hurry!" Ginger cried. "Just *hurry*, that's all!" And she floated out the front door and over the snow as if on skis.

"They're coming!" she called, forgetting to look at the car that was unwrapped now and standing in all its tan splendor. "Tim and Spark Plug are coming!" Then she hugged her mother and father again, the hood of the car and Shadow, and went skidding about in the snow.

The noon Christmas dinner was postponed. The turkey was covered with a blanket of aluminum foil; the potatoes were jerked off the stove before they had begun to boil; the big dish of scalloped oysters was slapped in the refrigerator until baking time, along with the salad and mince pie.

Ginger was no help. She tried to set two more places at the table, but her feet wouldn't stand still. The sheets and blankets she put on the beds in the big room above the garage went on at such crazy angles that her mother sent her out. She did manage to pick up the Christmas paper scattered about the living room and relight the big tree that stood in the bay window. Then she took the green hand-knitted suit her Aunt Maggie had sent her and dashed upstairs to try it on.

Dresser drawers were left in a sad state while she rummaged for a dark green blouse she was sure she had, and by the time she was dressed she decided not to wear the suit after all, so changed back into her red skirt and comfortable red sweater. Even a trial run in the new car with her father didn't last long enough. Though she had figured out that the drive for Spark Plug and Tim would take five hours on a vacation-packed turnpike, she hoped they could make it in four and a half, and fretted and watched the clock. Then, oh, wonder of wonders, she heard a horn making a fearful racket in the driveway and went tearing out through the garage.

This visit, though all too short, turned out to be more satisfactory than the one the "twins" had made late in August. The three of them toured the countryside, first in Tim's car, then in hers, and it was late in the afternoon of the day after Christmas when they tramped snow into a drugstore miles away and ordered hot chocolates.

"Let's take this booth," Spark Plug said, pulling Ginger out of her coat and hanging it on a hook, then Tim's, then his own. And as he started to slide in beside Ginger, he said, "There's a girl back there at a counter who looks like that Valerie De Camp you introduced me to."

"Where?" Ginger leaned around him to see. "Why, it is Valerie," she said. "She's exchanging something for a manicure kit." And she called, as she never would have done two months before, "Hi, Valerie. Merry Christmas."

"Well, Merry Christmas," Valerie answered, leaving the

counter and walking between the tables. "What are you doing way over here?"

Ginger was sure Valerie had seen Spark Plug and Tim before she started over, but she grinned and answered, "Out riding in the new car Santa Claus brought me." And she said, "You met Spark Plug last fall, and this is Tim Ford. Valerie De Camp."

Tim slid out to stand in the aisle with Spark Plug, and Ginger was sure Valerie looked longingly at the place he had vacated. "Sit down," Ginger invited, thankful to be found with two boys, not two girls.

Valerie's amazing violet eyes were focused on Tim. She had quickly discounted Spark Plug for two reasons. One, he wasn't extremely good-looking, and, two, he had made it plain last fall that he belonged to Ginger. Valerie had learned a hard lesson that day when Burke walked off after Ginger, so she was taking no chances. Today, sitting with two college students, one so handsome he made her wish she had worn her new leopard coat, Valerie felt great respect for this quiet girl who attracted boys without trying.

Valerie was able to see today, Ginger noted. Her hair was brushed straight back and hung carelessly, and apparently Valerie liked what she saw.

"Thanks," Valerie said, sitting down and leaving room for Tim beside her. But Tim squeezed in beside Ginger and left Valerie to Spark Plug. I suppose he wants to look at me, she thought complacently, knowing how pretty she was, even in old clothes and with her hair any which way. And smiling straight across the table at him, she asked, "Are you home for the holidays?"

"No," Tim answered. "We're visiting Ginger-cookie." And he said in a blunt way that was most unlike him, "She doesn't have much fun at Paxton Hill. What are you people over there doing to our favorite girl?"

"Why—why, nothing," Valerie stammered. Then she searched for a better reply, and said, "We live in such scattered directions, you know. When school's out we never see each other. I've felt awful about it because I'm supposed to be Ginger's big sister—every new girl has one—and I haven't done anything for her." She leaned forward and smiled directly at Ginger this time. "I'm having a crowd in tonight," she said. "Would you all like to come?"

Tim could feel Ginger's shoulders stiffen. Her fingers gripped the thick mug of hot chocolate that had been set before her, so he had to say before she could speak, "It sounds good. What do you say, Spark?"

Spark Plug was also thinking of Ginger. He knew this invitation could open up a social life for her, and his only question was, Did she want the boost because Valerie was making a play for Tim? "If Ginger wants to go," he said carefully, "it's okay by me. We have some other tentative plans, but if she wants to go I don't see why we can't cancel. What do you say, Ginger?"

"I don't know." Ginger realized that both Tim and Spark Plug were eager to do whatever they thought might help her. Spark Plug was willing to give up visiting a tremendously large bowling alley that he had promised Styx to see and report on; Tim was letting himself in for an evening that would bore him to death. "I think we can," she said, not wanting to make a definite acceptance until they could be alone and talk it over. "If we can cancel our other plans, that is. Will it be all right if we call you and let you know?"

"I really should know now," Valerie answered, aware that

she would have to rush home and frantically telephone as many of the Paxton Hill seniors as she could reach on short notice, even some of the juniors if she had to.

"All right. Then we'll come."

Tim and Spark Plug nodded agreement. But when they reached home they went off to their room to set up a secret plan. They would give Ginger an organized rush, they decided, with one or the other always watchful. Tim would be especially nice to Valerie, but he would let it be known that Ginger came first. And whenever a local boy hunted Ginger up, they wouldn't move in. It was to be her evening all the way, and together they would see that it was. Solemnly they shook hands on their pact; and, outwardly gay, they went off on a call to duty that neither would have chosen.

Ginger thought about the effects of that evening long after faithful Tim and Spark Plug had gone. She was invited to parties and even gave one. And although she couldn't understand whatever made her do it, she showed Valerie the small sister fraternity pin Spark Plug had given her for Christmas. Valerie had begun driving home with Ginger after school, for news of Tim, Ginger was sure, but her interest sparked the others. The senior class began to value its newest member.

So winter passed slushily into spring, and spring burst into glory. Ginger drove her car to school, and one girl or another often came home with her. She had named the car Joy, but for some reason she called it "he." "Poor Joy," she would say, "he can't take us to the Malt Shop this afternoon because I have to give him a wash."

Her grades were excellent; and, owing to the long months

when she had had nothing to do but study, she stood first in her class and was appointed to be valedictorian at the commencement exercises. Standing up in her home room and refusing the honor was the most difficult moment of her whole year.

"I'm very grateful," she found herself saying, looking from one to the other of her classmates, "but it wouldn't be fair for me to accept it. I've only been in the school a year, and my roots aren't here. I don't know the school the way the rest of you do. And while I've come to love it. . . ." She stopped and said, smiling, "I really have, even though I hated everything about it at first. Nothing was one bit like Cheltham High, and I didn't fit in. I didn't," she repeated, "so you didn't want me here."

There were shouts of denial, but she stood there shaking her head. "It wouldn't be fair," she said, "and you know it wouldn't. Hal Friedendorfer has the best grades next to mine, and he's been here ever since he was a third grader. He's the one who should be valedictorian, not me. Please believe me and support my decision with the faculty."

She sat down amid shouts of protest, but the class finally agreed, and Hal Friedendorfer became the one to write a speech that would make his parents proud and glad that they had sacrificed to send him to Paxton Hill.

"I had to do it," she said to Spark Plug on the telephone, just as she had explained to her class and her parents. "I'm not Paxton Hill and it would be wrong to pretend I am. I couldn't stand up before a lot of parents and eulogize my alma mater the way Hal can and will. I'm helping him with the part of his speech about what the future means to us, but he'll have to write the part about the past himself."

But she did take great pride in the yearbook. It was thicker than usual, and she had worked tirelessly on it. The articles were hers whether she signed her name to them or not, and she had skirmished about for jokes in the lower classes, chosen the illustrations, contributed one short story, and hounded the students who didn't bring their copy in on time. She and Burke had taken the unwieldy mass to the printer, edited the galley and page proofs, and had refused to give out a book to a student who didn't pay his five dollars in advance.

The junior-senior dance was of necessity a small affair when compared to the crowd that always filled the gymnasium back at Cheltham High School, but she did manage to get there in a new white net dress because, this time, George stayed healthy.

Sometimes she wondered what had become of her ulcer. It gave her no trouble, so she decided it either had healed or never existed. Dr. Randolph said it had healed, and pronounced her cured. And while nothing was quite the way she wanted it to be, and no fancy graduation in a garden could compare with the one she had always dreamed of having, sitting on a stage with a hundred and twenty-four other young graduates, it was better than she had dared hope for.

"Ah me," she said to her mother and father, sitting once more on their porch they loved so much, "here goes another phase in my life. Next year it will be college, and after four years of that what will I do? Go on and specialize in something?"

"Time will tell you, child," her father answered. "Just take it a year at a time. This year has been a long, tough one but you weathered it, and the others will seem shorter and shorter as you go along."

"Yep," Ginger said, contented now to live where she lived and do what she did. "It doesn't seem any time at all, really, since Spark Plug and Tim went off to college, and they'll be juniors next year. Golly, time does fly." And she got up to let Shadow in.

CHAPTER THIRTEEN

"HERE I am, the sweet girl graduate."

Ginger came out to the porch in her black cap and gown. She walked carefully, as if the mortarboard might slip sideways on her shining curls, and held her arms out stiffly, like a doll. "I feel like a nut," she said.

The rented gown had been pressed so that it hung in soft black folds; the tassel of the mortarboard dangled correctly over her left eye.

"Hm," her father said, inspecting her judicially. "You look fine, but I still don't see why you couldn't graduate from high school in a white dress, with the boys in navy-blue jackets and white slacks, as they do at home. I think it's much prettier."

"But not for dear old Paxton Hill," Ginger returned, making a face. "Old Mr. Paxton would turn over in his grave at the suggestion, and Mr. Hill—if there is a Mr. Hill somewhere in Europe, as I've heard there is—would come hustling home. Nope, this is the way they've done it for twelve years and this is the way they'll do it until the buildings crumble and fall down. I don't care much for it either, but I'll go along with it, the way I've had to accept all the other stodgy ideas the school perpetrates upon its helpless youth. How does that sentence hit you," she asked, catching her breath, "coming from a young lady who is about to be graduated? Do I dare sit down?"

"Heavens, no!" her mother cried. "Do you think I want to press that horrible black thing again?"

"Then find your hat, your purse, your gloves—but not the camera, please. It's bad enough to have to look like this without running across a picture of myself in the years to come. Oh, *please*," she wailed, as her father got up and opened his camera case. "It would be as embarrassing as seeing a photograph of yourself as a baby on a bearskin rug. The baby can't protest, but *I* can. For college? Yes. For high school? Definitely, no. I'm not going out in that yard."

The tinkle of the telephone saved her. It had a way of doing that, she thought gratefully, racing off to answer it, the tassel on her cap flopping.

"Oh, wait a minute, whoever you are," she pleaded, shoving back her long black sleeves so she could pick up the receiver. "Hello?"

"Hi," Spark Plug said. "I found I could get a plane home with a stopover in Washington, so here I am."

"Where?" she asked, unable to believe him.

"At the airport. Can you come and get me?"

"Oh, *yes*, I'll be right there. No, I can't." She had a previous and important engagement and she couldn't be late for it. She had to graduate. "Oh, dear," she said, and fell into the desk chair any old way.

Her gown wrinkled under her, her cap hit the back of

the chair and tipped down on her nose, and she had to say, "I'm late. I can't come."

"Is Tim around to come for me?" Spark Plug asked, hoping he sounded casual; and she took more time out to laugh.

"He's in college, I suppose," she said. "He sent me some red roses but he isn't here. Oh, Spark Plug, what shall we *do?*"

"Just leave the keys in one of the cars and I'll take a taxi to your house, then go on to the school. I'd have called sooner," he explained, "but this was an extra plane they put on for the college rush and the darned thing didn't stop in Pittsburgh."

"Oh, that doesn't matter, you're here." Spark Plug was coming to her graduation! Ginger took off her cap and laid it on the desk. "Oh, dear buddy," she said, afraid she was going to cry and ruin her face. "Oh, dear, dear, dear buddy."

"Now, keep calm." Spark Plug knew as well as she did that this was no time to become emotional, so he said, "You just leave the keys and I'll get there in time to watch you walk down the aisle."

"I don't walk down an aisle, silly," she said. "It isn't a wedding."

"I wish it were."

He mumbled the words but she heard them. She also heard her mother calling, "Ginger? For goodness' sake, come on!" "I'll tell you what we'll do," she said, getting up and trying to smooth out her gown. "We'll leave the Sprite at that gas station on the corner of Lilac Road and Main Street. It's quicker for you."

"Okay. Good luck."

She stopped at the powder room to run a comb through her curls and set her cap back on, then sped through the house. "You can take the picture now if you want to," she called, wanting to give her parents pleasure.

But her mother answered from the garage, "There isn't time." And from eavesdropping she added, "We'll take it with you standing beside Spark Plug when we come home. Daddy's gone on to the service station with the Sprite, and I'll drive your car. Now, be sure you sit down carefully."

The garden behind the main building of Paxton Hill looked lovely, Ginger thought. It wasn't a garden, really, but just a lawn under old shade trees, with a cleared space where the graduating class would sit before a long rose trellis. The Pep Club had been responsible for all the arrangements, and by delegating mothers to pitch in and help had managed to be ready on time.

Rows of folding chairs had been brought from a mortician's for parents and guests; students would sit on the grass; and over at one side a long tea table was set up. Its lace cloth belonged to Valerie's mother; one of the two silver tea services had been polished and brought over by Mrs. Johnston, and the cups, saucers, and plates of cookies and cakes had all been transported by other hurrying mothers that morning. Ginger, sitting in the middle of a semicircle with sixteen other black crows, decided that this was a rather nice way to do things.

The minister from the Presbyterian church gave a short invocation; Dr. Cartwright presented awards and diplomas; the valedictorian rose and cleared his throat; and, clutching a small silver vase and a medal she had received for being the most outstanding student, Ginger felt the hot afternoon sun beat down on her head.

She couldn't see Spark Plug, but then she couldn't see anything much, she thought, facing a yellow ball of fire that dodged in and out among the tree leaves. All she knew was that she was a very warm alumnus and that it was time to stand up and sing "America, the Beautiful."

The ex-seniors began talking to each other, some even solemnly shaking hands as if they might never meet again, as perhaps they wouldn't, and it seemed natural now for Ginger to be one of them. Valerie made her promise not to lose touch; Burke pumped her hand with heartfelt gratitude that she knew he meant. Betsy, Cecelia, George, all of them crowded around her at last, and she began to feel as if this really were her school and that she had never gone to any other.

"It's queer, but I'm kind of sad," she said to Spark Plug, after she had kissed her mother and father and guided them to the tea table, where they were happily chatting with other parents. "I'm actually loving this place."

"It's because you won out," he told her. "You came here unknown and unwanted, and in one year you won the most coveted medal the school has to give—'the most outstanding student award.' Doesn't that tell you something about yourself?"

"It tells me that it was a heck of a year," she said, taking off her mortarboard and wiping her hot forehead. "But I guess it was worth it."

"It was, if you look at your folks," Spark Plug said.

Mrs. Johnston held Ginger's diploma and the vase; Mr. Johnston was opening and closing the velvet box that held the medal as people asked to see it, and they looked so proud that Ginger felt a little catch in her throat. "I'm glad

I didn't let them down," she said softly, "but I do wish we could go home where I could tell them so in the cool of our own back porch."

It was more than an hour before they could leave. Ginger had to tell each of her teachers good-by, running about through the trees to find them and thank them for all they had done for her; and she saved her dear Herr Doktor Liebermann for last.

"I'll never forget you," she said to him in German, "and I'll take every German course my college has to offer. *Auf wiedersehen, Herr Doktor.*"

"*Auf wiedersehen, liebschen,*" he answered. "I have watched you, and you have given me my greatest triumph since coming to America. I pray you will continue to overcome all obstacles."

"Like a mountain climber," she said, impulsively kissing him on both of his round cheeks as a favorite German niece would have done. "Thank you, Herr Doktor."

She and Spark Plug drove home in the Sprite. Its midget top was down, and the air fanned her hot cheeks. "I loved every minute of it," she said, as they reached the entrance gate, "but just let me get into shorts. Uh-oh, what's that I see in our parking space?"

"Tim's car," Spark Plug growled, unconsciously slowing. "I had a hunch that that dumb crumb would try to make it."

He wanted to slam on the brake and shoot into reverse, but Ginger read his mind and said, "Don't you dare take me back. It was sweet of Tim to come, but just so you won't be jealous I'll show you something. Stop here."

Spark Plug's foot pressed down, and he watched Ginger

unsnap the top of the long gown that covered her summer dress. "There," she said, pulling it back. "Take a look."

The small fraternity pin he had given her was fastened to the white piqué of her dress, right above her heart "I've only worn it this once, where nobody could see it," she said, "so don't go getting any ideas that it's a permanent decoration. It isn't."

"But you wore it! Today, on this big day of days, *you wore it.*" Spark Plug shoved the little car into gear again with such happy energy that they almost left the gravel.

It seemed to him that they flew the rest of the way up the driveway; and coming to a jolting stop he was able to grin at a forlorn Tim who sat on the front steps with only Shadow for company.

"Sorry, old boy," he called, "that you got here too late and missed it." Then he gave Ginger's hand a squeeze, and confessed, "Dear buddy, I told a lie. I'm not sorry at all."

About the Author

Janet Lambert, beloved author of girls' fiction, was born and lived many years of her younger life in Crawfordsville, Indiana. Her hometown has been the home to many well known writers such as General Lew Wallace, author of Ben Hur. Prior to writing novels, the beautiful and talented Ms. Lambert performed as an actress and play writer touring with a repertory company around the United States and on Broadway. Her acting career was shortened during WWI by her marriage to then Captain Kent Lambert and later by the birth of her daughter, Jeanne Ann. As a perceptive and intellectually curious Army wife, Ms. Lambert gained insight into people, situations and life in many settings. These experiences were integrated into her writing for many years to come.

Janet Lambert's work has had and will continue to have a positive influence on the lives of "her girls" whom she loved so much.